# THE MARRIAGE LIST

## Jean C. Joachim

### Moonlight Books

This is a work of fiction. Names, places, characters, and events are fictitious in every regard. Any similarities to actual events and persons, living or dead, is purely coincidental. Any trademarks, service marks, product names, or named features are assumed to be the property of their respective owners, and are used only for reference. There is no implied endorsement if any of these terms are used. Except for review purposes, the reproduction of this book in whole or part, electronically or mechanically, constitutes a copyright violation.

**A Moonlight Books Novel**
Sensual Romance
THE MARRIAGE LIST
Copyright © 2011 JEAN C. JOACHIM
Published by Moonlight Books
Cover Art Designed by JK Cohen
Edited by Katherine Tate

# Dedication

FOR MY AUNT, NAN EDELSTON Cohen, who would have loved this book had she lived to read it.

# Chapter One

ENVY BURNED IN GREY'S chest as he walked through the door at Blondie's, the sports bar on West 79th Street. His three best buddies had it all, great jobs and great wives, while at 30 years old, Grey was still working night and day, saving every penny and sleeping alone...most nights. Tonight he faced the challenge of listening to them brag without letting the smile slip off his face.

The bar was beginning to get noisy with baseball games on three TVs and rowdy laughter. Grey wondered when it'd be his turn for happiness. He got a table and downed a drink before his friends arrived, brushing a careless hand through his sandy hair.

His hazel eyes swept the room for eligible women. There were a couple at the bar, talking to each other, looking pretty hot. Later, he'd try to drum up some action. One looked over at him, her gaze moving over his body slowly and her broadening smile indicated she approved of what she saw. Her blonde hair and ample chest made it hard for him to turn his gaze back to the door, where Will was entering, followed by Spence.

Grey raised his hand in greeting to his buddies as they made their way to his table. This was their quarterly get-together for a couple of beers and dinner. Though they were eight years out of college, when they were together it was like old times hanging at the fraternity. Practically inseparable in college, they called themselves the "Four Horsemen". When Bobby arrived, they motioned to the waitress for another pitcher of beer.

After placing their food orders, the Horsemen settled back in their chairs. Grey opened the conversation.

"So how's married life treating you guys?"

"Thinking about tying the knot, Grey?" Bobby asked.

"That would be news," Will put in, before taking a swig of beer.

"Yeah, yeah, 'Grey Andrews, tired of screwing different women every night sets the date'" Spence said, making quotation marks in the air with his hands.

"I'll drink to that," Will said, raising his mug in a mock toast.

"You'll drink to anything!" Bobby piped up.

"So who is she?" Spence asked, narrowing his eyes and gazing at Grey.

"No one. There's no one," Grey said, his shirt collar feeling suddenly tight. He reached up and unbuttoned his shirt then took a deep breath.

"Sure, sure. You don't have to tell us, but we'll find out eventually," Will said.

"Come on, guys, I'm serious," Grey continued.

"So you've stopped working sixty hour weeks and sleeping with whatever you could pick up at a bar?" Bobby asked.

"Maybe."

"Gonna kick out your roommate and squeeze a wife into that cramped place you live?" Will asked.

"I'm looking."

"So the nest egg is fat enough now, got enough cash and you're ready for the next step? Grey, you plan like a girl," Spence chuckled and the other two laughed with him.

"So marriage isn't so great for you guys, huh? Is that what I'm hearing?" Grey said, smirking.

Grey, the only unmarried one, wanted to hear how married life was treating his friends. Although he wasn't in love or even dating one woman exclusively, he was thinking about taking the plunge himself...time to start looking for Ms. Right. Spence was right, Grey was a planner.

Will took a gulp of his beer before he turned to Grey.

"Your crazy job giving you time off to get married?"

Grey had spent the past eight years working sixty hour weeks to achieve success; his job at an investment firm kept him busy watching his clients' money and his own. He lived on practically nothing, took girls on inexpensive dates, shared an apartment, all to save up for freedom and marriage, the way he wanted it.

"Still the master of the cheap date, Grey?" Spence asked him, putting down his empty beer glass.

So what if he was inventive enough to master the art of low-cost dating: picnics in Central Park, free concerts, trips to the Bronx Zoo on free entry days, long walks. The women he escorted didn't mind that dates with him were unusual instead of costly. Grey wooed his women on as few dollars as possible, saving every cent and it was paying off as he watched his money grow, multiplying at a rapid rate.

"I'm still careful with my money, Spence. How's your marriage, by the way?" Grey asked, lounging back in his chair.

Grey was on a mission, gathering data, information, formulating his plan for wedded bliss. After two pitchers, tongues started to loosen up.

"My wife is a pain in the ass with her decorator and her cook. The living room is white, can't wear shoes there. Can't put my feet up on the coffee table. And food! Tiny portions, salads. Give me a good meatloaf any day, I eat like a rabbit," Will complained, refilling his glass.

The table was silent for a moment.

"Bobby, how's that sexy lady you married?" Spence asked, his eyes glittering with either desire or envy, Grey couldn't tell which.

"Watch it, Spence. Just because she has big boobs..."

"Man, she must be hot," Spence continued.

"I said watch it!" Bobby got halfway out of his chair before Grey put a hand on his arm to stop him.

"What's the matter, Spence, not getting any?" Bobby teased.

"Susan's a great talker. She loves to talk. Very smart. Intellectual, in and out of bed. But the action I want in bed doesn't involve talking," Spence said, gazing down at his beer.

"I wish Tiffany would talk a little more. She says lawyer stuff is boring. I tell her 'yeah that lawyer stuff is what pays for your wardrobe, honey' but she doesn't get it," Bobby said, signaling the waitress for another pitcher.

Grey didn't hear anything like what he'd expected. He had steeled himself to hear enough bragging to make a strong stomach retch, but it never materialized. Instead his friends continued to complain about their wives, what their seemingly perfect wives lacked and what the Horsemen were missing. His frustrated pals killed his taste for the women at the bar and the discovery of their dissatisfaction caused Grey to wonder if married life was a good idea for him after all.

THE NEXT NIGHT HE WENT out to dinner with his sister, Jenna. She was two years younger than Grey and engaged to be married. Jenna taught middle school. The objective of her trip to New York City was to buy a wedding dress as well as to break bread with her favorite brother. Grey took Jenna to a nice French restaurant. After a good day in the stock market, he wanted to treat his baby sister to a superb dinner. Grey ordered a martini while Jenna had Chardonnay. She looked around at the chocolate brown walls with cream trim, the cream tablecloths and pink and white dishes and sipped her wine.

"How are you feeling about...uh...getting married?" He asked her.

"Great! Bill is everything I've always wanted in a man," Jenna cooed.

"Is he a good listener?" Grey said, opening the menu.

She nodded.

"A good provider?"

"He makes a good salary as corporate counsel for the bank." Jenna glanced at the list of specials on a separate sheet.

"And...in the sack...?" Grey asked, turning his gaze from her face back to the menu as he was embarrassing himself.

"Grey! That's none of your business...what we do in private. Honestly!"

"I know, but are you...ah, compatible?" Grey lifted the menu higher to hide his blush.

"What do you mean?" She put her menu down and stared at her brother.

"You know what I mean, Jenna. Stop playing with me," Grey insisted, dropping the menu.

"If you would stop asking such a personal question..."

"Compatible...like you both want it the same all the time, uh, most of the time."

"Grey! I can't believe you asked me that." Jenna looked to the left and right to see if anyone at a neighboring table overheard him and was staring at her. She was relieved to find the other patrons were absorbed in their own conversations, not paying attention to her discomfort.

"Are you?" He put the menu down, enjoying having his sister on the spot.

"I'm not going to answer. Why are you asking me these personal questions? It's not like you," Jenna said, color rising in her cheeks.

"We had a 'Four Horsemen' meeting two nights ago."

"You still keep in touch with those guys?"

"Sure, they're still my best friends."

The waitress appeared and they ordered dinner. Grey picked a wine to go with the meal and gave the waitress the once over. Jenna shot him a dirty look and he smiled back sheepishly.

"And? Your dinner with the Horsemen?" She prodded, picking up her water glass and taking a drink.

"They were talking about their wives...complaining actually, each about different things and I've been thinking. I wouldn't want to trade places with any of them. I used to think they had it all...great jobs, great women," he cleared his throat, "now I'm not so sure."

"You don't want to fall into the same trap?"

"Each one had a separate complaint, a completely different thing bugging him about his wife. Three big things." Grey looked down at his hands.

"One of them was s-e-x?" Jenna raised an eyebrow.

"Spence," He added with a wry smile, "Not getting enough. I wouldn't want to have to beg my wife to sleep with me." Grey picked up his water glass, drinking while he watched his sister.

The waitress returned with the wine, popped the cork and filled their glasses. Jenna waited until the waitress was out of earshot before continuing the sensitive conversation.

"That's why you're asking me all these personal questions?" Her face lit up with understanding.

"I need to know if it's standard...after you're together for a while...begging?"

"Did Bobby and Will complain about that?"

Grey shook his head.

"So then it's not like that with everyone." Jenna took a sip of her wine and smiled her approval.

"Translation, you and Bill are sexually compatible. You don't make him beg?"

"Only if he's been a bad boy," she laughed.

"Jenna! Get serious." He coughed, choking on his water for a second.

"How can I? This is ridiculous. Do you even have someone you're considering marrying?"

"Not yet, but I will. I plan to. Things are going well for me now and soon I'll be in a position to have a new life, one with room for a regular woman."

"A regular woman? I'd hate to think of you with an irregular woman," she snickered.

"Jenna! You know what I mean."

"Andrews family bachelor is thinking about settling down. That is news."

"It's not a joke," he complained, refilling their wine glasses.

"I'm sorry, Grey. I know it isn't. Lord knows you're not getting any younger...seriously, I'm glad to hear it."

The waitress arrived with their food.

"I need help here, some guidance," Grey said before putting a fork-ful of sole meuniere in his mouth.

"Let's begin with the way I solve almost every problem in my life...with a list," she said, digging in her purse for a pen.

"I'm not into lists...it's a girl thing."

"Do you want my help or not?" She pulled a small pad of paper out of her purse.

He nodded, then waved his hand for her to continue.

"Okay. Three guys. Three frustrated husbands. Three wifely flaws. First one?" She asked cutting off a piece of chicken cordon bleu.

"Bobby complained that his gorgeous, sexy-as-hell wife wouldn't listen to him. She thought his legal work was boring. I want to be able to talk to my wife about whatever business I'm in, whether she has big boobs or not," he said, breaking into a grin.

Jenna gave him a stern look.

"Number one, she should be smart. Able to talk and listen," Jenna said, writing, "next?'

"Will said his wife is spending all his money on decorators and cooks yet he doesn't have a house he feels comfortable in. The guy holes up in a den, smallest room in his giant house, because Vicky's decorated the whole house in white and it gets dirty...or something like that."

"Translating Will's problem into a wish...for your wish list."

"Not a *wish* list. This is a *'must-have'* list," Grey said, taking a hefty portion of sole on his fork.

"All right, so how do you translate Will's dilemma into a quality you want?" Jenna took the opportunity to have another bite of her dinner.

"Hmmm. Not so easy."

"A homemaker?"

"Sort of. I'm not looking for Betty Crocker here...someone who can manage a household, I guess...and create a nice, comfortable home for me, since I'm pretty stupid at that. And who can cook herself. I don't want to hire a decorator or a cook. Does that make sense?" He asked.

"A woman who can decorate a house, make it comfortable, right? Not a showplace, without bankrupting you and can cook a decent meal," Jenna said, scribbling on the pad.

Grey nodded his head in agreement.

"The third thing...Spence?" Jenna asked.

"This one is important. No begging for sex," Grey finished the last bit on his plate.

"Sexually compatible, right?"

"More than that."

"How so?"

"She's gotta want it as much as I do. I don't want a woman who turns her head to the side and says, 'okay, go ahead', I want one who is eager for it...for me...who wants...I can't discuss this with you, Jenna," Grey said, picking up his wine glass to hide his blush.

"Write this last one yourself. I'm putting down sexually compatible, whatever that means to you. Please *don't* explain it to me. Okay?" Jenna asked, tearing a sheet of paper from the pad.

He smiled a wicked grin and nodded in agreement with her.

"Here is your list. Memorize it. Every time you go out with a woman, you look for these three things," Jenna advised, stuffing the paper in his breast pocket.

"What about honesty? Sense of humor? Looks?" He raised his eyebrows.

"Those are important traits, especially the first two. I assume everyone has to have those to get to the second date with you anyway. The list is for more than two or three dates. Use it when you consider spending a lot of time with a woman. That's when the list kicks in. I gotta go," she said, looking at her watch.

"No dessert?"

"Not if I want to get into the size eight wedding dress I bought today."

"Thank you, Jenna," he said, kissing his sister on the cheek.

"You may think it's silly but women make lists...all women have a list they use on men, too, a list just like yours. Use it, Grey. I hope it helps you find the woman you're looking for."

"Me, too," he said, dropping some bills on the table and walking out of the restaurant with his sister.

GREY AND JENNA KEPT the list to themselves. They never spoke about it to friends or family and rarely discussed it with each other. As time went by, Grey found he valued the list more and more, as it seemed to save him from one bad relationship after another. He never got in too deep when he remembered the list and found a woman wanting in any of the characteristics on it. He felt grateful to the list for saving him from a broken heart or an unhappy marriage.

Neither Jenna nor Grey imagined such a small list could eliminate so many women. Grey intensified his search but after three years found he still didn't have a wife, fiancée or even a woman with serious potential. He was lonely and frustrated, racking up financial gain with no one to share his good fortune.

He refused to abandon the list which became imprinted on his brain, the little piece of paper long discarded. He still believed it would lead him to his true love, but after searching for what he considered a long time, this patient man was finally growing impatient.

# Chapter Two

UPTOWN ON MADISON AVENUE, Carrie Tucker walked quickly down the long hall from her tiny office at Goodhue, Walker and Beane Advertising to Mr. Goodhue's office. She unbuttoned the top two buttons of her blouse, tossed her streaked blonde hair, made a face and buttoned up the lowest one again.

Called in to see Mr. Goodhue usually meant one of two things: promoted or fired. She had received praise for her work as a junior copywriter for two years, which lead to her promotion to copywriter. After two more years as a copywriter, was she going to be promoted to senior copywriter or get fired? Her nerves made her sweat, she felt dampness under her arms. As Carrie rounded the corner past the reception area, she unbuttoned again and kept walking.

As she neared his office she mumbled to herself, "This isn't a beauty contest," and buttoned up again, just in time to stop in front of Mr. Goodhue's secretary.

"Good morning, Wanda," Carrie said, training her clear blue eyes on the young woman.

"Hi, Carrie. He's waiting for you, go in," the chubby, brunette with the biggest, bluest eyes she'd ever seen said.

Carrie took a deep breath and walked in.

"Carrie, sit down," Nathan Goodhue, graying at the temples, dressed in a perfectly tailored custom-made Italian charcoal gray suit, motioned her to a chair. He sported the white shirt and red tie that senior management was often required to wear, company colors.

She took a seat and tried, unsuccessfully, to smile.

"Something wrong?" he asked, looking down at her from his full six feet two inches.

She shook her head, crossed and uncrossed her legs.

"You're not afraid of me, are you?" He asked, trying to hide a grin.

"Are you going to fire me, Mr. Goodhue?" Carrie blurted out.

"Goodness, no!" He laughed and sat down behind his desk.

Leaning forward, he eyed the beautiful young woman, took a sip of coffee from the Limoges china cup on his desk, and cleared his throat.

"You've done an excellent job her at GWB. I want to thank you by giving you a chance to show your stuff," Goodhue said then leaned back in his chair.

A sigh of relief escaped from Carrie, then she waited for him to continue.

"You know that the fastest way to become a creative director here is to bring in new business."

She nodded.

"I'm giving you a shot at it by putting you on the new business team."

"New business team?"

"In addition to working on the Country Lane Cosmetics account, you will now be working with Gus and Joanne on new business pitches."

"That's a lot of extra work isn't it?" Carrie crossed her legs.

"It does entail some nights and weekends, but I understood you wanted the fast track. You *do* want to be our first female creative director, don't you?" Goodhue sat back and clasped his hands behind his head.

"Well, I had hoped..."

"This is the way to get there...the only way. All our creative directors have been instrumental in bringing in an important piece of business. Then they run it."

"It's kind of like doing another job at the same time, isn't it?" Her grip on her cup tightened.

"It's more work, but you don't become a creative director without doing more than others. Creative directors must show stamina as well as spark and talent. Are you hungry enough? If you are...if you want it, you won't have a problem with a little extra work." He stood up and returned his cup to the credenza.

"But I understand it's much more..."

"Have a boyfriend who will object?" He turned his head and spoke to her over his shoulder as he refilled his cup.

Carrie shook her head.

"So what's the problem? I know three other copywriters who would give their right arm for this chance. You have more talent than they do. That's why you're getting this opportunity, first, Carrie. Take the ball and run with it." Goodhue returned to his desk and flipped up the screen on his computer and opened his calendar.

The interview was obviously over. Carrie was stunned. She stood up, realizing she was expected to leave. "Thank you, Mr. Goodhue, for the vote of confidence."

"You're welcome. You've earned it, my dear. Now prove me right," he said, lifting his head up to speak with her then returning his gaze to his screen again.

Carrie walked out of his office, pasted a small smile on her face for Wanda, and continued down the hall. When she got to her office, she closed the door and plopped down into her desk chair.

*Great, more work but no more money! Some honor. Be honored to have no social life. Still, I could become the first female creative director at GWB, something I've been working toward for the past seven years.*

Carrie wondered how much more work would be involved. She had watched other copywriters burn out trying to keep up their regular workload and create brilliant new business pitches at the same time. Many quit when the pitches didn't produce the big accounts they dreamed of. Now she would be in the hot seat. *It's an honor to be chosen, isn't it?*

Her thoughts were interrupted when a pretty, well-dressed, dark-haired woman stopped at her doorway.

"Lunch?" she said.

"Big news today," Carrie said, smiling up at Rosie Carrera, Assistant Production Manager.

"Give!" Rosie said, entering the office and closing the door behind her.

"Mr. Goodhue just asked me to join the new business team." Carrie leaned back in her chair and rested her feet on her wastepaper basket.

"I hope you told him 'no', right?" She said, sinking into a modern chair across from Carrie's desk.

"You don't turn down Mr. Goodhue. Come on." She sat up straight in her chair.

"He's the big cheese. But you don't want to do it, do you?"

"I want to be a creative director...so I guess I have to do this."

"I thought you wanted to write?" Rosie asked, raising an eyebrow.

"This is writing."

"I mean more than advertising stuff...real writing."

"This is real writing," Carrie said, leaning back in her chair.

"I mean...I mean fiction."

"That's my true love, but I can't support myself on that and Prince Charming isn't scheduled to stop at my house anytime soon, so I'm on my own."

Carrie didn't want Rosie to know she had finished a novel, a mystery, she'd written in the evenings and on weekends when she was between boyfriends.

"You give up too easily on men."

"Do I? Is there one self-centered creep left in New York I haven't gone out with yet?" Carrie scoffed, taking a sip of her coffee then making a face when she realized it was cold.

Rosie laughed, "Probably not."

"You took the last old-fashioned Prince Charming, Rosie and the rest of us are jealous," Carrie said, grinning at her friend.

Rosie blushed. "Yes, Eduardo is my Prince Charming. But I still have to work...just for a little while longer."

"Then you can quit and have a baby," Carrie said, diverting her gaze out her nineteenth story window to the sky.

"You'll have that dream someday, too, Carrie."

"Glad you think so. I've given up."

"Given up? You're only twenty-nine...crap!" Rosie scoffed.

Gus Parker opened Carrie's office door and stuck his head in. "New business meeting in ten minutes, Carrie...small conference room."

He was gone as quickly as he'd come.

"So much for peace and quiet...and lunch today," Rosie said, getting up.

"So it begins," Carrie said, standing up and stretching her arms above her head.

"Enjoy this roller coaster ride, you asked for it," Rosie said smoothing out the wrinkles of her skirt before heading back to her office.

"I did, didn't I?" Carrie said, rummaging around her desk.

After Rosie left, Carrie pulled out a fresh notebook from under a pile of papers, tucked it under her arm. She twirled a pen between her fingers as she walked down the hall. *Getting the chance you've been dreaming of can backfire. What if I'm not good enough?* She chewed on the end of the pen as she approached the small conference room.

# Chapter Three

HER PALMS WERE SWEATY, her heart was beating rapidly and her mouth went dry. Carrie was about to face her first pitch on her mystery book to an editor and she was scared, scared shitless. She entered the small room set aside from the rest of the writer's conference for editors to meet with writers. A short man in shirtsleeves and wearing nondescript, brown horned-rim glasses sat behind a desk. *He must be Paul Marcel, editor for Rocky Cliffs Press.*

Carrie straightened her skirt and made sure her blouse was slightly unbuttoned but not too revealing. She picked up her manuscript and synopsis and walked in, feeling anything but confident. She sat down across from him and smiled.

He smiled back and looked down at a printed sheet. "You're Carrie Tucker?"

She nodded.

"Tell me about your book," he said, sitting back, folding his hands together behind his head, watching her.

Just as she was about to open her mouth, a man strode into the room.

"Paul! Wait. We need you in the conference room," the man said.

"I'm just about to hear a pitch, Grey, can't it wait?"

"Sorry, John is only here for an hour and if you want that loan..."

Paul looked at Carrie and smiled again.

"Miss Tucker...Carrie, I'm sorry but we're going to have to reschedule this pitch. I have a meeting with an investor I can't put off," he said, looking down at the papers in his hand, "I have your contact info here. I'll get in touch to reschedule."

With that, Paul marched out of the room with the man he called "Grey" right behind him. Carrie stood up and put her hand on Grey's arm.

"Hey! You ruined my opportunity to get my novel published! I've been waiting six months for the chance to see Paul Marcel," she shot at him.

Grey turned. His gaze swept over her hair, eyes and figure making her feel slightly naked and yet warm at the same time. She stared back boldly at the handsome man with a dazzling smile and an impeccable gray suit, noticing how snugly his suit fitted his trim physique

"Give it to me," he said, reaching for her manuscript, "I'll make sure he reads it."

Before she could move, snatched the manuscript out of her hand and walked quickly out of the room. She trailed along behind him, trying to speak, but soon he was lost in the crowd.

*What happened here? Where's my manuscript and who was that guy?* Carrie found a cup of coffee and a chair. Everyone was rushing around, looking for various lectures and rooms where they were meeting with agents, editors and publishers. She watched the bustle die down as people found their places. She sat there wondering what she was supposed to do now. Her manuscript was gone and she had no interest in the workshops, lectures and marketing panels addressing attendees. Carrie looked at her watch, four thirty p.m., an entire vacation day squandered on this opportunity. She might as well wait a while to see if Paul Marcel reappeared.

By six o'clock, most of the people had cleared out. Workers stacked chairs and collapsed tables. Famous authors chatted among themselves as they packed up and moved toward to the door. Still no Paul Marcel. But the good-looking guy wearing a gray suit who grabbed her manuscript came into the center hall, looking around. He spotted her and sauntered over.

"Glad you're still here," he said, his eyes looking directly into hers.

"And?" she said, trying to ignore the little shiver running up her spine.

"I gave your manuscript to Paul and he promised me he'd read it tomorrow."

"Why should I believe you?" She asked, noticing how broad his shoulders were but trying to keep her gaze on his face.

"Because I'm the silent investor in his publishing house. He wouldn't lie to me. I'm Grey Andrews," he said, offering her his hand.

"Carrie Tucker," she said, losing her small hand in the warm, dry flesh of his powerful one.

"Carrie, I'm gathering information on ebook publishers now. Would you be willing to join me for dinner and tell me what you know about ebook publishing, from an author's point of view?"

*He's smooth, gotta give him that.*

"How do you know you want to talk to me? I might be new to this business."

"I read some of your book, your synopsis and biography. You're a good writer, can't be that new."

"An advertising copywriter, not the same thing," she corrected him, fascinated by the wry grin on his perfect lips.

"Maybe not. But the work of yours that I read...was well written. You'll probably get published and be pretty successful at this."

"So you want my opinion?" She asked, impressed he had read her work.

"If you don't mind. Can I pay for it with a nice dinner?" He asked, moving closer.

"Why not?" She agreed, feeling warmth in her body growing as he neared.

"How about Le Chien D'Or?" he asked, mentioning a chic French restaurant, located on West 55th Street.

She smiled at him as he took her elbow and guided her out of the Hilton Hotel where the meeting was being held and toward the restaurant only a few blocks away.

CARRIE DIDN'T KNOW if she was disappointed Grey Andrews spent the entire dinner actually grilling her about ebooks, publishing and her dreams as a writer or not. She blushed a few times under his scrutiny and when his hand brushed hers reaching for the cream, the tingle went all the way up her arm.

She thought they had chemistry, but when he took her home, he didn't make a pass or ask to come up for coffee. He didn't even kiss her goodnight! It felt weird to be out with such an attractive man and only talk business.

*Maybe he's gay.*

"You've been very helpful, Carrie. Thank you. I'll make sure Paul reads your manuscript and gets back to you."

She nodded and went in the door, puzzled.

*Win some, lose some.*

Carrie shrugged her shoulders and flipped on the radio as she went to the bathroom to brush her teeth. She found herself dancing to Michael Bublé's "Haven't Met You Yet."

# Chapter Four

THE NEXT DAY AT WORK, Dennis, her supervisor called her into his office.

"I haven't seen much of you lately," he said, leaning back in his chair.

"New business," she said, as she slid into a chair facing his massive desk.

"Great. Country Lane Cosmetics had just been put into review."

"What?" Carrie sat forward, her eyes widened.

"The client is looking at us along with three other agencies."

"Oh my God, why?"

"There's a new president...he favors a different ad agency. He brought a new ad director with him. She likes us but doesn't have the final say. The account is in jeopardy, Carrie...and so is your job."

"What do you mean, my job?"

"You're the head copywriter on Country Lane. Most of your salary is paid by the fees from this account. If we lose it, there goes the money to pay you. Get it?"

Carrie sank back into her chair and scowled. *One minute I'm going for creative director, the next I'm almost out the door!*

"Don't make any plans for the next two months, Carrie," Dennis told her.

"But I have new business work, too."

"Yeah? If we lose this account, you won't be here to do new business. Your new business will be looking for a job. If we lose an account, heads roll. And this time yours is on the chopping block with the rest of us."

"Tell me what you want me to do."

"I want you available twenty-four seven. Tell new business to take a hike."

"I can't do that. Mr. Goodhue put me on the team."

"Then don't plan on getting much sleep," he said and stood up.

The meeting was over. She got up and left his office thinking about how quickly her opportunity to advance might vanish into thin air. Then she wondered how she could work any more hours than she already was. It was bad enough that her work as part of the new business team kept her there a couple of nights a week and at least one weekend a month, now with this extra load, she'd never have time to write...or to date. She would remain alone.

Worry about her job preoccupied her mind until she got home and heated up a frozen dinner. Taking her plate and a glass of wine out onto her tiny terrace, Carrie sat and gazed out at the huge city before her, thinking about her non-existent social life. She knew men found her attractive because she had no trouble finding men to date, but none of them were right for her. If they weren't jerks, being immature or selfish, then the chemistry was lacking. Then this guy, Grey Andrews, came along, with fabulous chemistry, and he was probably gay. No man, maybe no job...she felt discouraged.

The phone rang and she managed to grab it before the answering machine went on. She took the cordless phone out on the terrace and sat down.

"How's my favorite niece?" Delia Tucker asked.

"Ha ha, I'm your only niece, Delia. That is getting pretty old by now."

"Sorry. It's a habit. What's up? I haven't heard from you in a while. Working hard or occupied with a new man? I'm hoping both."

"I wish, I wish. No man. Just work and maybe not even that for much longer..."

ACROSS TOWN, GREY ESCORTED his sister, Jenna, out to dinner. She was in the Big Apple to go shopping, visit a museum or two and attend the ballet with her brother. Tonight, Grey loaded Jenna in his silver Jaguar XK and drove her down to Chinatown to his favorite Chinese restaurant. He reluctantly parked his convertible on a side street.

After they were seated at their table, Jenna opened up conversation.

"We're a little worried about you, Grey," she began.

"Hmm?" He mumbled, pouring out two cups from a steaming pot of hot tea.

"You're not getting any younger. What are you now? Thirty-four? And no wife in sight, eh?"

"Chopsticks?" He asked his sister, offering her a pair.

"Fork," she said, making a face and putting the chopsticks aside.

"Jenna, just because you and Bill are happily married, doesn't mean everyone can be so easily. I've been looking, believe me."

"Are you still holding tight to your *list*?" She asked, stirring a little sugar into her tea.

"I told you, the items on the list were not negotiable." Grey opened the menu.

"So have you met anyone who fits yet?"

"A woman I met this week meets the first criteria. Can I order for both of us?"

"Which one is that? Nothing weird, okay?" Jenna sat back into the red vinyl booth.

"She's smart. Very smart. A writer."

"Good. Maybe she'll be smart enough to figure out how to win you over."

"I'm easy, Jenna. I told you..."

The waiter returned and Grey ordered fried dumplings, sesame chicken and scallion pancakes. The waiter nodded, smiled and left.

"So this woman has made it past step one?"

"That's not uncommon."

"If you would only compromise..."

The sesame chicken arrived. The waiter also deposited two small bowls of steaming white rice on the table.

"Why should I? Those are three simple wishes to fulfill. Those are my keys to marital bliss. Without them, I cannot be a happily married man, so why should I even bother?

"Sometimes you can be infuriating," Jenna said, scooping rice onto her plate.

"Determined. Determined to have my way in this." Grey piled the sesame chicken on a small pile of rice in his plate and dug in, deftly moving the food from the plate to his mouth with chopsticks.

"Make your own rules and I hope someday you find this elusive mystery woman who is as good in the kitchen as she is in the bedroom," Jenna said, picking up her cup of tea.

Grey grinned and motioned the waiter for a check.

"If I find her...when I find her, you'll be the first to know."

"I believe *you'll* be the first to know, Grey," Jenna laughed as she clinked her glass with his.

Grey dropped some bills for the tip on the table and took the check up to the cash register. Jenna returned from the ladies room and the two climbed into his car and drove uptown.

# Chapter Five

IT WAS EIGHT O'CLOCK and the Upper West Side of Manhattan was quieting down from the traffic and honking horns of rush hour. Men and women were going to restaurants, curtains were going up on Broadway shows and Carrie was arriving home from work.

She felt tired from brainstorming on two new business pitches and working on a new product line for Country Lane Cosmetics. She barely had time to breathe and was now looking forward to settling in at home with a glass of wine, a frozen dinner and a good book.

Carrie locked the front door behind her when her cell phone started to ring. She groaned, sure it was Dennis from the office. Seemed there was always one last thing to tell her about some project or other. But the number on the phone display was not Dennis, in fact it wasn't recognizable to her at all. Curious, she answered it anyway.

"Carrie?"

"Speaking."

"It's Grey Andrews."

"Oh, hi."

"Have you heard from Paul yet?"

"Haven't but it's only a few days since you gave him the manuscript."

"I'll call him. He shouldn't keep you waiting."

"That's nice of you. Thanks," she said, moving to hang up the phone.

"Wait! Wait!"

"Something else?"

"I was wondering if you'd like to have dinner with me and go to the ballet on Tuesday night?"

*A date?*

"Is this business?"

"A date, actually."

"Oh...I'd love to. How did you know I liked the ballet?"

"I believe you made reference to it at our dinner last week," he said.

*Wow! A man who listens.*

"You'll have to pick me up at work, or I can meet you at the restaurant."

"I'll pick you up. Give me your address and I'll be outside in a car, waiting for you at six o'clock. Does that work for you?"

"That's fine. I have to go back to the office after the ballet..."

"Oh?" She could hear the disappointment in his voice.

"We're having a business crunch and I'm working long hours. I just walked in the door when you called."

"I'm glad you can carve out the time to come with me."

"Me, too. See you then."

"Goodnight, Carrie, pleasant dreams."

Carrie hung up the phone and plopped down on the sofa. She couldn't have been more surprised if she'd won the lottery. *So Grey Andrews isn't gay and he felt the chemistry as much as I did.. Called less than a week after our date. Hmm. Could be interesting.*

She got undressed, slipped into bed and fell asleep thinking about Grey.

"YOU'RE LEAVING?" DENNIS asked her.

"I have a date, Dennis."

"But we have so much work to do..."

"Not tonight. I'm going out. I'll work on it at home, better yet, I'll come back after the date," she said, packing papers into her briefcase.

"Joe's not gonna like this," he warned.

"Tough. I've got a life, too."

"Had a life, Carrie, had,"

"Speak for yourself," she said, pushing by him to get to the elevator.

Carrie was wearing an aqua silk dress, cut low and fitted at the waist that brought out the blue of her eyes. The skirt was full but soft and clung to her hips and thighs. The air was cool for August so she had a lightweight jacket thrown over her shoulders. When she hit the street, Grey stepped out of a black limousine and held the door open. When he looked at her, she felt his gaze like the caress of a warm hand sliding gently down her body.

"You look beautiful," he said, holding the door for her.

She smiled at him, watching his eyes, pleased to see the light of desire spark there when he looked at her. He was wearing a charcoal Grey business suit with a blue shirt and a black knit tie. Flecks of green in his eyes glittered when they looked at her. He took her hand, sending shivers up her arm, and helped her in the car then eased his six foot one inch frame in next to her. Their shoulders and thighs touched, making Carrie tingle. Grey gave instructions to the driver then took her hand.

The car stopped at a little French restaurant on Second Avenue called Sans Souci. The tiny place was charming, intimate and romantic inside, with about fifteen small tables, dark turquoise walls and red tablecloths that went all the way to the floor. A table in the corner had been set for two, with one tall candle glowing and a bottle of wine waiting. Grey held out her chair then sat down next to her, instead of across from her.

The Maîitre d' came by and placed napkins in their laps, and then asked for drink orders.

Carrie shook her head. "Just water, please."

"Are you sure?"

"I have to work after the ballet, so I need to be awake."

"Wine with dinner?"

"Maybe just half…okay one glass," she said.

"Tell me what is keeping you so busy," Grey asked, pouring the wine.

Carrie spent the next ten minutes regaling him about the stress of trying to save the Country Lane Cosmetics account and handle the pressure of new business assignments at the same time. He quietly took her hand and listened attentively.

"What about you? What exactly do you do and how did you get there?"

"Big questions…can't be answered in a few simple sentences. Let's order first."

Carrie ordered *coq au vin*, Grey, steak *au poivre*, then he began his tale.

"I worked like a dog for ten years to amass as much money as I could. I was lucky with real estate and other investments, very lucky. Now I'm an investor, a partner in a small company that backs new green ventures…like epublishing."

"That's admirable. Do you work…like a regular job?"

"Not all day everyday anymore. We have a small staff and every quarter we select a company to invest in. The rest of the time we spend researching, interviewing and meeting with principles in new start-up companies. When we have a company we're serious about, work can get intense with long hours and many meetings. I find it exciting helping new companies. We have slow time, too. Sometimes I spend days and days doing nothing but research…"

"Can't imagine you stuck with a computer or a stack of papers and not out talking to people."

"I am a people guy but every business has its downside. Tell me more about you."

"For instance?" She asked.

"Do you cook?"

"For one? Rarely."

"If you were...uh...more than one, would you cook?"

"Depends. Maybe."

"What kind of home life did you have as a kid?"

"My parents were successful. We never wanted for anything, except their time. They were always busy, we fended for ourselves...you've heard of latchkey kids?"

"Siblings?"

"A brother. You?"

"A brother and two sisters."

"Oldest?"

"No, second. Have an older sister."

"Close to your family?" She asked.

"Very. You?"

"Not so much. My parents live in Arizona, my brother in Chicago."

"Did you celebrate holidays, have family traditions?"

"Why all the questions? This feels like a job interview..."

He looked down at the tablecloth and blushed.

"Sounds like an interview for a wife," she continued, her keen eyes searching his face.

"How do you feel about family? Want one? Want kids?" He went on.

"Kids? Absolutely. Home life? Have always wanted to create the one I never had. Hoping to have a Currier & Ives Christmas some-day..."she said, rather wistfully.

He grinned.

"And you?" She asked, turning her gaze on him.

"I want it all," he said simply.

"The whole thing? Picket fence 2.3 kids, two-car garage..."

"Kids, Christmas, house...everything...except maybe the white picket fence...with the right woman," he admitted.

"So...is this a job interview for a wife?" She persisted.

He took a sip from his wine glass.

"Getting to know you, that's all. I take a keen interest in all my dates," he said, sidestepping the question.

She eyed him suspiciously when the waiter arrived with their food.

"All your dates? And am I one of many...hundreds...thousands?" she teased.

He laughed. "Right now, you're the one and only." He put down his glass and his gaze met hers.

*Good and let's keep it that way.* She grinned at him.

GREY WATCHED CARRIE dig into her food enthusiastically and felt happy he'd invited her. Obviously she needed a good meal. He watched her face while they ate. With her eyes on her food, he could study her without detection. Her oval face had smooth, delicate skin with a slight blush in her cheeks. Her nose was straight and grown-up looking, not one of those baby-face noses sculpted by a plastic surgeon, her chin was strong but feminine. Her honey hair with streaks of light blonde curled slightly around her face softening her look. He was enchanted by her natural beauty.

"This is delicious," she said, her mouth half full.

He laughed. "Take it easy, no need to rush. We have plenty of time."

"I'm starved. Do you want a taste? It's incredible..." she offered.

He nodded. She picked up her knife to slice off a piece for him, but he put his hand down over hers, stopping her.

"Like this, from your mouth," he said, leaning over and gently placing his lips on hers. His tongue barely skimmed the surface of her lower lip, then her upper lip, tasting the sauce still lingering there. Gently his lips coaxed hers open and his tongue dipped in just far enough to share the taste of chicken on hers. She closed her eyes.

Carrie didn't move, except for her chest, which heaved with her rapid breathing, as his tongue took one last gentle swipe over her lips then he sat up.

"Ummm. Delicious," he said, feeling his pulse return to almost normal and a

slight tingle in his lips as he sat back in his seat.

As she sat there staring at him, color started at her face and spread all the way down her

Chest. Grey smiled at her, staring into her eyes as she sat, touching her bottom lip with the tip of her tongue.

"No teasing me, now," Grey whispered, glancing at her tongue. He returned his attention to his own meal, picking up his knife and fork, slicing off a piece of meat and putting it in his mouth.

Grey tried to concentrate on the meal, but his eyes kept seeking hers, his gaze drifted to her cleavage more times than he wanted to admit, even to himself. Watching her lips consume the chicken gave him lustful thoughts. He wanted to touch her in the worst way. Grey was a seasoned single man, one attractive woman should not affect him like this, disrupting a wonderful meal that passed into his stomach totally ignored by his taste buds, which were mentally tasting Carrie instead.

"What?" She asked.

"Like to look at a beautiful woman," he murmured.

*She could be it. The one.* Just the idea made him nervous with anticipation. *Don't jump the gun. You've been close before. But I want it to be her.* Delightfully, she was quickly making progress on his list. Her interest in creating a home intrigued him. But could she, would she want to do it on her own? Much about Carrie remained to be seen but he especially looked forward to exploring the last item on the list with her. He obsessed about her sexual appetite, crowding all other thoughts out of his mind. Would they be sexually compatible? It was all he could think about. The trick was not to start exploring that idea while still in the restaurant.

Chewing on the last piece of chicken, she looked at him again and cocked her head.

"Nothing. It is a crime to admire you?"

"It's a *little* more than admiration, Grey. I feel like your eyes are burning a hole in my...in my..."She blushed.

He simply had to touch her.

"I'll behave," he interrupted, pushing a lock of hair away from her face.

"Good."

*Is that a strike against her? She doesn't want to flirt or be sexy with me? We're in a restaurant, maybe she's a private person and if we were alone...maybe she would...*

"More wine, Monsieur?" The waiter asked.

Grey shook his head and raised his eyes to hers just in time to catch her looking at his lips. *Ah, too soon to call.*

They finished dinner and returned to the car which would take them to the ballet. They had twenty-five minutes before curtain time. Grey was out of patience denying his libido. He pulled Carrie into his arms for an ardent kiss. He started slowly, nibbling on her lower lip, while his hand rested on her neck, his thumb feeling her pulse quicken. He worked her mouth with his tongue. Her arms wound around his neck, pulling her closer to him as a soft moan escaped from her mouth. Her response fueled his desire. The more she melted in his arms, the more he wanted her.

The kissing got intense and his hand moved up to her breast. He squeezed gently and she groaned, a little too loudly. The sound brought Grey back to Earth. He removed his hand and sat back. The chauffeur checked in his rearview mirror and blushed.

"I'm sorry, I shouldn't have taken...have...done that," he breathed, wondering if she could tell he was getting hard.

She nodded, trying to catch her breath, her gaze dropping down to her hands. He leaned over to whisper in her ear, "I find you so attractive...I can't help myself."

She reached up and touched his face, her gaze searching his. He saw disbelief in her eyes and wanted to reassure her.

"This isn't a line to get you into bed. We couldn't tonight even if you wanted to…I know you have to go back to the office after the ballet. I'm not setting you up. I find you…amazing. Is that bad?" He asked.

She pulled him down for a sweet kiss, which he deepened easily. She tasted so good and smelled fresh and sweet, like lilacs. He ripped his mouth from hers and took a nibble of her neck. She closed her eyes and moaned softly as his lips traveled down then back up her neck leaving soft kisses. Before he could make another assault on her mouth, the car came to a stop.

"We're here, sir," the driver said loudly, after clearing his throat.

Grey looked up, almost sorry to see they had arrived at the ballet. He sat back, straightened his tie and jacket while Carrie tried to smooth the wrinkles out of her dress and replenish her lipstick. The driver came around and opened the door.

"Handkerchief," she demanded, extending her hand.

Grey pulled out his handkerchief and handed it to her. She carefully and gently wiped the lipstick from his mouth and cheek, then handed the white cloth back to him. He smiled at her.

He maneuvered Carrie in front of him to hide his erection, hoping it would disappear quickly. His strong reaction puzzled him. He hadn't known Carrie long and though she was beautiful and sexy, his response was more than usual in this situation. His reaction to Carrie stunned him.

They got out of the car with Grey angling Carrie so she was blocking his private parts from view. He relaxed as they walked toward the door, fishing in his breast pocket for the tickets.

"I love the ballet. This will be so relaxing for me," she said, squeezing his arm.

*Not so relaxing for me, sitting next to you, wanting to touch you, forced to sit still and keep my hands to myself.*

CARRIE SLIPPED HER hand into Grey's, smiling up at him as she walked into the lobby of the theater at Lincoln Center. Her face was warm from their passion in the car; in fact her whole body felt tingly and alive. His touch, his lips were like magic and when he put his hand on her breast, she thought she was going to pass out as the fire of her desire seemed to consume her. If their destination had been twenty miles out of town, she knew she would have succumbed to him in the back seat with a stranger at the wheel. *How embarrassing, where's your self-control?*

Sneaking a sideways peek at him, she was proud to be with such a handsome man. His sandy hair flopping a little over his forehead made him look boyish even though his face was more mature. Still, he was devastating, smooth, sophisticated and sexy as hell. She enjoyed every minute with him.

They settled into their seats and he helped drape her coat around her shoulders, touching her bare skin, sending sparks down her spine. When the lights started to dim, he took her hand in his, lacing his fingers through hers as they sat back to enjoy the show.

Carrie didn't find it as relaxing as she expected. She couldn't seem to get comfortable in her seat, perhaps because Grey was occasionally stroking her palm with his thumb, which kept her in a constant state of subtle arousal. She shifted again and heard the person behind her make a cluck of disapproval. Finally, she smiled at Grey and got up, unable to sit still any longer. Out in the lobby, she pressed her hot face against the cool window, hoping to settle her core.

"Restless?" Asked a voice behind her.

She turned her head to find Grey right behind her and could feel his hands on her waist.

She nodded.

He leaned over and planted a light kiss on her neck. When she turned around, he pulled her to him for a sweet kiss that grew passionate immediately. Reluctantly, she pushed him away.

"Not helping."

"Who said I was trying to help?"

She laughed, then covered her mouth, not wishing to disturb those watching the performance in the theater. He took her hand and led her over to the coat check area, finding an alcove there with a pay phone. He pulled her into the alcove against the wall and pressed hard against her body as his mouth found hers. She fell into his arms, softening against him. The kiss grew passionate. She moaned softly and whispered in his ear,

"Touch me,"

He responded immediately. His fingers closed around her breast while his other hand slid down to her bottom and squeezed, then pulled her up against him. She ground her hips into his and felt his erection, making her gasp slightly. His hand massaged her breast, seeking the nipple, which he gently pinched. They were so wrapped up in each other, they didn't hear the applause as the ballet broke for intermission. Even the sound of approaching footsteps did little to stop them. Carrie managed to pull her mouth away as she heard the tapping of a foot on the floor. She peered around Grey's shoulder and saw the man standing still and frowning at them.

"Get a room. This is the ballet, for crissake!" he muttered as he walked away.

Carrie buried her flushed face in Grey's shoulder and moved her hips back from his. He put his hand in her hair, brushing it down and kissed her cheek.

"Sorry, but..." he whispered in her ear.

"...it takes two," she said.

He smiled and stepped back from her, waiting a minute or two before taking her hand and joining the intermission crowd, keeping her in front of him. Carrie went back to her seat and snatched up her coat.

"I can't focus on this...the performance...with you next to me," she whispered in his ear.

Grey saw a few people staring at them and knew the man with the frown spread the word about them to others, so he accompanied Carrie out of the auditorium with an amused grin on his face. Once in the lobby, he took out his cell phone and called the car.

A few more people stared at them as they walked down the hall and Grey felt his face flush. Carrie started to giggle when she heard people whispering and noticed the stir their rapid exit was making. By the time they reached the front door she was dissolved in laughter and so was he. The chauffeur opened the car door. They laughed all the way back to her office.

When the car pulled up to the curb, they were both wiping their eyes.

"At least we weren't undressed," she said.

Her comment started another fit of laughing. When they both quieted down, Carrie gathered her coat, purse and briefcase and turned to Grey.

"It was an amazing evening, Grey. Thank you so much."

"Even if we practically got kicked out of the ballet?" He joked.

"Dinner was fabulous and the ballet was...stimulating?" She said, snickering.

He took her in his arms and kissed her.

"Goodnight, Carrie. Don't work too hard," he said, smoothing her hair with his palm. Grey sat in the car and watched her walk into her building, the car pulled away when she was safely inside.

# Chapter Six

CARRIE DIDN'T WORRY about hearing from Grey again. Anyone who was all over her like he was would be back for seconds...and more. She focused on her work, though it took her a half hour to come down from the high of the best date she'd had in years.

At two o'clock, she called it quits and called a car service. She was in bed by three and up again at eight, dragging herself back to the office. Dennis was there, pleased with her work and loaded with more for her to do. She planned to stay there Wednesday and Thursday nights until very late. The call came on Wednesday morning at work. Harried, hassled and preoccupied, Carrie answered the phone in a gruff voice.

"Hello!"

"That's not the soft voice purring in my ear last night."

"Grey?" She smiled, picturing his sexy smile and laughing eyes.

"Can't stop thinking about you and it's screwing up my work day, Honey. Can I take you to a Yankees game then dinner this Saturday...seats on the first base side?"

"Saturday?" She asked, pulling out her calendar.

"Please say 'yes' so I can get back to work. I'm losing money!"

"I have to work. But I can sneak out for a few hours," she said, holding the phone very close for privacy.

"The game starts at 2 p.m. I'll send a car to pick you up at 2:30. I'll be waiting outside when you get here."

"Wonderful! The new Yankee Stadium?" Carrie sank down into her desk chair.

"None other."

"I love baseball...but I suppose you remember than from our conversation."

"I'm a good listener."

"Such a rare thing in a man," She said, putting her feet up on her trash can.

"I have an excellent memory, too. I remember some other things about you...things that need pursuing."

Carrie blushed at the tone of his voice.

"See you Saturday, Grey," she said and hung up when he finished chuckling.

Carrie sat back for a few moments, enjoying the idea of being with Grey again. Dennis burst her romantic balloon by putting his bulky self in her doorway and clearing this throat.

"What's this about Saturday? We're working Saturday."

"I'm coming in early, leaving at 2:30 and will return at eight if I need to. I'm going to see a game at the new Yankee stadium."

"Good seats?"

"First base side."

"I suppose, if you're coming back and all, its okay. Wish I could go with you."

Carrie smiled and kept her mouth shut rather than tell Dennis how glad she was he wouldn't be there.

That night as Carrie climbed into bed to read for a few minutes her phone rang.

"I'm not interrupting anything...by any chance, am I?"

"Delia! Of course not. I've been working long days there is no chance to interrupt anything," Carrie chuckled, putting the book face down on her stomach.

"That's not good, Carrie. You need a man in your life. You should be thinking about marriage," Delia said.

Carrie scrunched down in the bed.

"Right now I' thinking about holding on to my job."

"Oh, right, right forgot about that. When am I going to meet this man of yours?"

"He's not mine and I have only seen him a couple of times. He's taking me to a baseball game and dinner on Saturday," Carrie said, her voice soft.

"How cozy! Are you going to bring him up for coffee?"

"Aunt Delia, Uncle Jackson would be appalled at your questions."

"Are you?"

"I have to go back to work Saturday night."

"Maybe that's not so bad. With all the delay, by the time you two get together, there'll be real fireworks! Sleep tight, Angel."

Delia hung up the phone and Carrie put her book away. She shut off the light and lay in bed, thinking about when she'd finally get time alone with Grey. She didn't think long as she was asleep within ten minutes.

TIME SEEMED TO FLY by and Saturday came quickly. It was a delightfully sunny, pleasant day in September. Carrie dressed in boot cut, light blue jeans, with a raspberry-pink long sleeved tee shirt with a scooped neck. The outfit showed her trim figure off to perfection. Navy tennis shoes, some casual jewelry and a denim jacket to protect against the cool evening air completed the outfit.

She headed out to the office at eight a.m., unable to stop smiling. When she arrived, the other members of the team greeted her with grumpy hellos. As they hid behind huge cups of Starbucks coffee, Carrie fairly sang out her 'good mornings' and beamed at everyone.

They got down to work quickly and she kept focused until 2:15. Grey was a stickler for being on time and she knew the car would be waiting outside in fifteen minutes on the nose.

In the ladies room she replenished her blush and lipstick and added mascara and some light eyeliner. A dab of her favorite lilac cologne for her signature scent.

"Hope the Yanks win," Dennis said as she went into the elevator.

The ride to Yankee stadium was quick with little traffic on a Saturday. Carrie sat back and watched the boats on the Hudson River as the car sped up the West Side Highway toward the Bronx. The gleam of sun off the water reflected on the trees and flowers in Riverside Park. A feeling of happiness washed over her as she sank back into the comfortable seat.

The driver made a quick call as they turned off the highway and when he pulled up to the stadium, Grey was waiting outside for her. He scooped her up into his strong arms for a huge hug and kiss before taking her hand and leading her into the stadium. She looked around, unable to decide if the new stadium looked more like an office building or a modern prison. She gave a slight nod as the notion of a huge bank came into her mind.

Carrie was almost blinded by the bright green of the grass as she followed behind the tall, slim man all the way down almost to the front row half way between home plate and first base.

Just as they sat down, Alex Rodriguez put the ball out of the park. The cheering was deafening and Grey took the opportunity to pull her into his arms again. They jumped and yelled and laughed.

Once in their seats, Grey offered her food.

"The new stadium has a ton of new kinds of food. You can have the traditional hot dogs and beer or soda or something fancier. They have barbecue, Dunkin Donuts, even salads. What's your poison?"

"It's still the ballpark...gotta be hot dogs and soda."

"Turkey Hill ice cream?

"That's the best!"

"I had that as a kid upstate, but how do you know Turkey Hill?"

"I travel," she said blushing.

"Some guy introduced you to it, didn't he?" His eyes narrowed.

"Maybe...Look, Jeter's coming up to bat."

Grey took the hint and dropped his inquisition about her past. He plied her with hot dogs, soda and ice cream. He drank beer. Grey had come from work, too. He sat next to her with a baseball cap pushed back on his head, gray slacks and a blue striped, long sleeved shirt with the sleeves rolled up to his elbows. His tie had been pulled loose and hung limp a few inches below his collar. Several buttons on his shirt were released to reveal a bit of his chest hair. Carrie wanted to reach inside his shirt and flatten her palm against him. She felt her pulse take a quick leap.

He pointed out the special features of the spanking new stadium, leaning in close to her. Her eyes followed the line of his arms and finger pointing, but she couldn't concentrate with him so close to her. His scent enticed her and she could feel the masculine heat radiating from his chest so near hers. When he sat back, she gazed at him. The casual cap, the shirt sleeves revealing his powerful forearms lightly covered in sandy-colored hair. His broad shoulders and chest pulled a little at the shirt. She guessed he was probably not a perfect fit for one size but was actually between two sizes. His handsome face glistened with a little sweat in the sun. Carrie felt her pulse quicken again and heat begin to course through her veins just looking at him and yet she couldn't look away. She wanted him.

"Look, he's going to steal third...it's a hit and run play," Grey said, pointing to the player taking a huge lead off second base.

Just as he said it, the runner on second base took off and the batter hit a single to center field. The man on second scored and the crowd went wild. Grey leaped up with the rest, yelling and raising his hands over his head. He pulled Carrie out of her seat and enveloped her in his arms. She ran her hands up his chest as her eyes made contact with his. He looked down at her and lowered his lips to hers. She wound her arms around him and pulled them closer. Grey deepened the kiss but soon everyone else sat down. Fans started to catcall the kissing couple. Someone whistled, then he was joined by two or three others clapping and whistling, too.

The fans around them laughed while Carrie was mortified. They sank back down in their seats and settled for holding hands until the game was over. About five thirty they made their way to the parking lot and Grey's silver Jaguar XK.

"For dinner, since we're up here already, I thought I'd take you to Arthur Avenue."

"What's Arthur Avenue?" She asked, turning to face him.

"You grew up in New York and don't know that the real Little Italy is on Arthur Avenue in the Bronx? Best Italian food outside of Italy and the bakeries...wow!" He put the car in gear and they wended their way down side streets filled with children playing, radios blasting, people sitting on stoops, playing cards, boom boxes broadcasting songs in foreign languages. They drove past block after block of three and four story brownstones, some colorful, some red brick and some the traditional brown.

Grey found a parking space in front of Firenze a small Italian restaurant. He opened the door for Carrie and escorted her inside.

There were a dozen tables squeezed into the tiny restaurant. The walls were dark green and each table sported a Chianti bottle with a candle burning in it. They were early and the place was almost empty. Carrie ordered the ravioli and Grey had the chicken *parmigiana* with spaghetti.

"How was work today?" Grey asked, cutting off a piece of chicken.

"We're working on three new approaches for this one client. Sometimes I get confused because I'm working on too many different things at the same time. You worked today too, right?"

The ravioli seemed to melt in Carrie's mouth; she had never tasted pasta so good.

"Susan and Max like to run their research by me before they present it to John. John was my boss. When he retired he decided to start this business and he brought me along. Of course I had to kick in equal start-up money, but that wasn't a problem."

"How did you make all your money?" Carrie blurted out, then blushed at the boldness of her question.

Grey looked at her and laughed.

"I'm so sorry. That was rude of me. Please, forget I asked."

"It's okay. I bought townhouses to start with."

"Townhouses?"

"To save money I used to take my dates on lots of interesting walks. We'd walk up to Harlem and back. I noticed gentrification was beginning to move North, so I looked into buying a few townhouses, renovating them and selling them at healthy profits." Grey took a sip of his red wine.

"Pretty smart," Carrie said, cutting another piece of ravioli in half with her fork.

"Guess so. I also bought one for myself and kept it."

"You live in a townhouse?" she asked, her eyes wide.

"Uptown. It isn't big, but it has enough space for me...and for...the future," he said, coughing, "I made a ton of money that way and then I invested it in carefully researched companies...companies I was watching for my clients. I made about twenty percent each year."

"Someday, if I become a creative director, will you invest my money for me?"

He chuckled. "How about I teach you how to invest and you can do it yourself?"

"I like that idea," she said, smiling as she wiped her lips with the napkin.

Grey turned his wrist to look at his new iPod watch.

"Almost the witching hour. Have to get a rain check from you on pastries for dessert."

*I have a completely different kind of dessert in mind for you the next time we meet.* She eyed his torso hungrily wondering what he looked like underneath his corporate veneer then nodded and smiled at him.

Grey drove her back to her office fifteen minutes before she was due. They sat in the car smooching like a couple of teenagers until she had to go in.

"I had a wonderful time today."

"It helps when the Yankees win," he said, playing with the car keys.

"Oh, did they win? I didn't notice," she teased.

"What?"

"I'm kidding. My wonderful day had all to do with you, silly," Carrie explained, opening the car door.

"I'll call you tomorrow," he said, when she closed the door.

"Good night."

"Good night, honey," he said, raising his hand.

Grey put the car in gear and roared away from the curb.

# Chapter Seven

ON SUNDAY, CARRIE SLEPT late, recovering from her six-day work week. At eleven o'clock, the phone rang.

"Good morning," came the smooth, deep voice of Grey Andrews.

"Good morning to you, too," Carrie's sleepy voice returned.

"Dinner Saturday?"

"Lovely." She stretched her arm above her head.

"Good. Rest up. I expect you to be able to stay awake for dessert."

"Maybe we should start with dessert first," she teased.

"Don't have to twist my arm," he snickered.

"Hmmm," she muttered, closing her eyes and picturing him naked.

"See you Saturday," he said and rang off.

SHE WORKED EVERY NIGHT until nine thirty. By Thursday Carrie was tapped out.

"I'm leaving early tomorrow," she told Dennis.

"Early? Who said?"

"I said. I'm exhausted, Dennis. Just one afternoon, geez."

"Okay, okay. You can leave at one tomorrow, but be here on Saturday."

"Saturday, again? No can do. I have a date. But I'll work at home on Sunday for a couple of hours."

"It's that damn new business stuff. If you were only working on Country Lane...but you're not. Your work is still good, Carrie. Okay, deal. Can't afford to have you get sick on me."

Carrie walked out of his office and down the hall, where she bumped into Rosie.

"How you doin'?" Rosie asked her, a look of concern on her face.

"Exhausted."

"You look it. Haven't seen you in weeks. Any chance you can take a few minutes for lunch today?"

"Lunch? I'm leaving early tomorrow, so taking lunch today wouldn't go over well. But I have to eat."

"I brought a sandwich. Come hide in my office and we'll eat," Rosie offered.

Carrie agreed, returned to her office and pulled up Country Lane project number 112 on her computer.

AT ONE O'CLOCK ON FRIDAY she packed up her briefcase to work at home on Sunday. A piece of paper slipped out of her agenda book and fell on the floor, right under her feet. She picked it up. It read it: "Mom's Beef Bourguinon Short Cut Recipe."

She tucked the recipe into her pocket and walked out. It was overcast with rain threatening, a chilly late September day in New York. She wrapped her raincoat around herself and walked to the subway.

The wind whipped down west 78$^{th}$ Street, blowing Carrie's hair in front of her face as she approached the brownstone that housed her apartment. Loaded down with groceries, Carrie could barely make it up the three flights to apartment. She dropped everything inside her front door and ran to shut the windows as the apartment was chilly. She put on music, unpacked the groceries and pulled the paper with the recipe on it out of her pocket.

"Okay, Mom, here I go," she said to herself as her favorite Michael Bublé song, "Haven't Met You Yet" came on.

The pre-heating oven warmed the whole apartment. Carrie undressed down to a comfortable shift and began to cook, sing and dance to the music. Cooking was fun for her, especially with her mother before the family got fractured with her parent becoming obsessed with making tons of money and working constantly.

Her mother and father had started a catering business together when they were both unemployed and Carrie was only ten. The business had taken off because her parents worked night and day to make it a success. Carrie was raised mainly by her grandmother as her parents were always cooking, supervising events and selling their services, especially during holidays. The more successful they became, the more driven they became, terrified of losing all they had acquired. At first, Carrie missed them terribly but soon got used to being alone. She never quite adjusted to being on her own during holidays and those days remained difficult for her even now.

Her one-bedroom apartment had a tiny fireplace in the living room. The small kitchen, tucked between the living room and bedroom was well-equipped. She laid out the meat, chopped mushrooms, cooked the bacon and opened wine, pouring a generous glass for herself.

At five o'clock she put the dish in the oven and sat down with her glass of wine to put her feet up. She was already feeling better. Then she realized Grey was expecting to take her out to eat on Saturday and she had cooked. She picked up the phone.

"Hi there," she said, when he answered before she took another sip of wine.

"Carrie? Saturday... You're not canceling on me, are you?" His tone became urgent and questioning.

"A change of plans," she corrected, sitting up straight putting her feet back on the floor.

"No dinner?"

"Dinner here. Okay?" She chewed her lip.

"Your place?"

"I found an old recipe of my mom's and decided to make it. It's in the oven cooking now...smells great."

"Hmmm. What is it?"

*"Boeuf Bourguinon."*

"I'm impressed and salivating already."

"Keep your pants on, handsome..." Carrie smiled and sat back on the sofa, putting her feet up on the coffee table.

"What made you think..."

"Tuesday night?"

"I'm salivating in that department, too."

She laughed. "Are you assuming we'll..."

"Not assuming anything here...but a guy can hope, can't he?"

"Tomorrow will be our third date." Carrie picked up her wine glass and took a sip.

"Our fourth."

"The first one was business," she corrected him.

"That's what you think."

"It was a date? You didn't even kiss me goodnight!" She put her feet down and sat up.

"Checking you out before puckering up."

She laughed.

"Same time tomorrow? Or do you want me to come over tonight and...uh...stay until tomorrow...then I'm sure to be on time," he chuckled.

"Good try. Six o'clock like we said and don't be late or I'll start without you..."

"Start what without me...oh...the food! I see."

She giggled, shook her head, hung up the phone, and got up to check the oven.

# Chapter Eight

BY FIVE THIRTY ON SATURDAY, Carrie put finishing touches on her makeup, and then she was ready. She wore a long-sleeved, cream-colored cotton sweater, low cut over skin-tight, stretchy jeans. Around her neck was an amethyst pendant that hung down almost to her breasts. She added the matching earrings and fluffed her hair.

The *Beouf Bourguinon* was in the oven, warming up. The aroma filled the apartment and seeped out from under the door, wafting down the stairs to fill the narrow hallways and tiny vestibule. The table was set with her best dishes, white with tiny butterflies and flowers in shades of lavender and light green. The small round table was covered with a lavender cloth to the floor, topped by a shorter one in darker purple layering the setting. The crystal wine and water glasses were shining and there was one silver candlestick with a light green candle perched in the middle of the table. *Pretty romantic, he might get ideas. He's already got ideas, I have to make up my mind what I want to happen.*

Carrie dabbed a little lilac perfume on her wrists and between her breasts. Just as she was putting the stopper back on the perfume, the buzzer to the outside door sounded. She looked at her watch, two minutes of six. She giggled to herself as she walked over to the outer door release button, surprised by the excitement bubbling up inside her.

AS SOON AS HE OPENED the wrought iron front door to the brownstone, Grey smelled the French stew cooking. *I hope that's coming from Carrie's place.* As he climbed the two flights of stairs, the aroma grew stronger and he felt his stomach rumble in response. He held an expensive bottle of red wine in one hand and a dozen red roses in the other. A smile grew on his face as he was pretty confident he'd get the chance to make love to her. He'd been thinking about Carrie all week, the taste of her lips, the feel of her breasts, the firmness of her butt. Being able to enjoy a baseball game together was icing on the cake. Unlike other women, she had crawled under his skin quickly, inching closer to his well-protected heart.

When she opened the door, she looked beautiful and he was right, the wonderful cooking smell came from her apartment. He kissed her lightly, handed her the flowers and stepped inside. Expecting to find, like every other woman her age, an apartment sparsely furnished in cheap furniture, his mouth fell open at what he saw. He walked into the living room and was struck by the beautiful red and orange striped matching loveseats on either side of the fireplace. An old cobbler's bench served as a coffee table between the sofas. An antique pine corner cabinet, shined to a gloss, hugged the corner while tan burlap curtains moved in the slight breeze that entered even when the windows were closed.

"Your apartment is beautiful. Did you do this?" His gaze traveled through the living room to the kitchen and down the long hallway to her bedroom.

"Do you mean, did I hire a decorator? Hell no, why would I?" she asked.

"Some people prefer to leave decorating to someone else."

"This is my home. I want it the way I want it. My taste. Can't leave that to someone else." Carrie handed him a corkscrew.

"I agree." He went to work on the bottle of cabernet sauvignon he brought.

"Did you decorate your own place?"

He shook his head. "I hired help. I didn't know where to begin," he said, embarrassed.

A timer went off in the kitchen, calling Carrie before she had a chance to respond. He noticed the round table romantically set for two and the French doors with gauzy white curtains. There was a straw rug, early American lamps, two throw pillows and some small pieces of art on the white marble mantle. A narrow credenza fit behind one of the sofas and held a beautiful basket filled with fruit. There was a small bowl of nuts on the cobbler's bench. He never expected to see such an enchanting apartment when she opened the door. He glanced down the short hallway toward the bedroom.

"Off limits for now…" she said, her eyes following his gaze.

"Can't I get a tour? I love what you've done, can I see the rest?"

"Sure, come on," she led him to the terrace which had a small dark gray wrought iron table and two with peacock-blue-cushioned chairs, also wrought iron. Then she took him down the long hallway turned into a mini-gallery for the original art hung there. There was an impressionistic pen-and-ink sailboat, two decorative plates in red with gold and turquoise highlights, a large mountain scene oil painting and several others he didn't have time to examine closely on his swift walk back to the bedroom. Carrie's bedroom walls were painted light sky blue andtrimmed in soft yellow. The bedspread was a country print in shades of blue, yellow and white. She had a small country French antique pine chest of drawers and white lamps on either side of the bed. He noticed the queen-sized bed and smiled.

"What's that for?"

"What?" Grey tried to change his smile to one of innocence but failed.

"The wicked grin on your face."

"Nothing, nothing, admiring your bedroom. It's a great room, nicely done. Can't I do that without an ulterior motive?"

"What do you like about it?" Carrie narrowed her eyes and turned to face him squarely.

"The décor...the colors...to be honest, the size of the bed tells me a lot about you."

"How so?"

"If it were a twin-sized bed, then I could be pretty certain we wouldn't be sharing it any time soon...a double bed means I have a 50/50 chance, but a queen-sized bed means..." he blushed, suddenly aware he was giving away too much.

"Means?" She prodded.

"Never mind," he said, moving toward the door.

She pulled on his arm and he turned.

"Means what?" She insisted. She blocked his path to the door and put her hand on her hips.

"Means you're interested in...spending some time with someone else in a bed big enough for two, especially a man my size."

"I see. Leaping to some pretty big conclusions here aren't you?" She put her hand over her mouth to cover a smile.

"Hope is speaking again," he said, pulling her closer for a kiss.

"Gotta get the dinner," she said, pulling out of his arms and moving down the hall.

Grey followed behind her, watching her sway as she walked, his desire growing. His heart began to beat more rapidly as he realized Carrie might be the one woman who met all three criteria on his list.

She arranged the roses he brought in a vase and put them on the coffee table, then stopped to give him a quick "thank you" kiss and returned to the kitchen. He stood in the living room looking around at the pieces of original artwork on her walls, each perfectly framed and artfully arranged, until he heard a scream, then a clatter. He ran into the kitchen to find Carrie clutching her hand, tears in her eyes.

"What happened?"

"Sometimes I forget...I picked up the pan without the mitt," she said.

Grey quickly and calmly reached into the freezer and grabbed a few pieces of ice. He took her hand, gently placed the ice on the burned skin and held it there with one hand. With the other, he took a small bowl out of the cabinet and filled it with cold water. Then he plunked the ice in the water and led her to the dinner table. She sat down and he put her hand in the ice water.

"Keep it there. I'll get the food," he said, kissing the damaged area before putting it in the bowl, wiping away a tear on her cheek with his thumb.

Carrie sat back, keeping her hand in the icy water. She watched Grey handle the casserole adeptly and get the noodles and salad to the table.

"You have experience, I see," she said, trying to light the candle with one hand.

"In a big family, everyone helps at mealtimes," he replied, removing the matches from her hand and lighting the candle with one sweep.

"Where did you grow up?"

"Upstate New York, in a small town...you've probably never heard of it, Pine Grove."

She shook her head.

"Country boy, eh?" Carrie put her burned hand back in the ice water.

"Easily transplanted to the big city." He returned to the kitchen.

"Ever get back home?"

"For every holiday." He raised his voice so she could hear him as he turned off the oven and put away the oven mitts.

"You're lucky."

"Don't you visit your parents?" He asked, sitting down at the table.

"They have busy lives. Sometimes I go at Christmas, but traveling then is such a zoo."

"What about your brother?"

"He spends time with them, it's not as far for him and he's a teacher, so he has the time."

He heard a tinge of sadness in her voice. A woman with all these talents and she wasn't married or engaged...or was she?

"You're not involved with anyone, are you?" He poured more wine.

"Would I be dating you if I was?" She looked up at him.

"I hope not."

"I'm available, if that's your question. I'm not seeing anyone...anyone regularly." She took a sip of the wine he brought and smiled her approval.

"To the cook, long life and much happiness," he said, bringing the glass to his lips.

She smiled and drank, too.

"Then there is someone else?" His head jerked up slightly as his eyes gaze made contact with hers.

"Not really. There were...uh...was. You didn't think I was sitting at home every night waiting for your call, do you? I had one or two men in my life when you came along."

"And now?"

"Now?" She blushed.

"Are you still seeing them?" He shook out the cloth napkin and spread it on his lap.

"Actually...well..."

"Well what?" He demanded, staring into her eyes.

"I'm not," she admitted, dropping her gaze to her plate.

"Good. I don't share," he said, taking his first bite.

"And you?" she asked, eyeing him keenly.

"You're my one and only now." Yesterday he'd decided not to call Monica again. Or Louisa either. He had no interest in either of them, or any other woman since he met Carrie.

"Now? I don't share either," She stated, raising an eyebrow.

*Whew! Close call. Never thought about her having another guy.*

"This is amazing," he said, closing his eyes, rolling the food around in his mouth for a few seconds.

"It's good, isn't it?" She cut the tender meat with the side of her fork, avoiding using her injured hand.

"God, it's more than good, it's incredible. You made this?"

"From mom's secret recipe." Her smile grew wide.

*She's got the first two on the list nailed, cold.*

He felt nervous and giddy, watching her come closer to fulfilling his dreams. No one else had come this close in a long time. It seemed finding a woman who could cook and create a tasteful home was like finding a four-leaf clover. He dug into the food, savoring every bite.

They ate in silence for a while, until Carrie swiped her tongue across her bottom lip to lick off some gravy. Grey watched her tongue and felt his pulse climb. She looked at his eyes, then dropped her gaze to his lips. She blushed when he smiled knowingly at her and focused on her food again.

When they finished, Grey got up to clear the table.

"How's your hand?"

"Much better, thanks." She said, looking at the red spots on the inside of her fingers.

"Stay there. I'll clear. Do you want me to stack them?"

# Chapter Nine

AS SHE WATCHED GREY move back and forth between the kitchen and the dining table, she couldn't take her eyes off his trim body clad in a simple sports shirt and gray slacks. His camel jacket was hung behind the front door. Her heart melted. No one had made a physical hurt better for her in so long she couldn't remember. He was sneaking into her heart too fast. With the stress and craziness at work, the last thing she needed was a love affair. Love took effort, energy, shaving your legs on a regular basis, time and attention she didn't have while her job was in jeopardy.

Try as she might, she couldn't resist Grey Andrews. Forget the chemistry, his sweetness, his generosity and his sense of humor were beyond resisting. *Can't forget the chemistry.* Once he got near her, touched her again, she knew she'd fall into his arms, giving herself to him enthusiastically. *Okay, I want him. This is crazy, insane. There's no time for him...but I want him.*

"We have lemon sorbet for dessert," she said, getting up as he sat down after clearing the table. "Want coffee, too?"

When she walked by, he stopped her by putting his hands on her waist, and pulled her into his lap.

"All I want for dessert is you," he whispered in her ear, sliding his hand under her hair, gently urging her face closer to his. His lips closed over hers in a sweet kiss. She put her arms around his neck. His tongue found hers and they played for a little bit. Carrie's breathing quickened as his left hand moved up over her sweater to capture her breast. She groaned softly, wanting more.

He massaged her breast, finding her nipple and ran his thumb over it, making it hard. Carrie softened against him, urging him on. His right hand reached around behind her and slipped under her sweater. He released her bra with one hand, then returned to her waist while the other hand dove under her sweater, under her bra to make contact with her naked breast. She gasped as his cool hand covered her warm flesh.

"Sorry," he muttered, removing his lips from hers for a quick second.

His hand continued to fondle her breast. He caressed it, squeezed it...thumbed and circled her nipple. His lips left hers and headed for her neck. His nibbled his way down her neck and down her chest, while he slowly slipped the shoulder of her sweater down until her breast was exposed to his lips, which devoured it eagerly.

Carrie was panting slightly, running her hand through his hair, closing her eyes. Heat filled her body, wetness pooled between her legs.

"I want you, Carrie," he whispered roughly.

She lifted his face up and stared into his eyes, her own smoky with desire. She kissed him, moving her tongue into his mouth, taking him, pressing her body against his. She wanted him, too, had wanted him for weeks. Then she pulled back.

"Make love to me," she whispered.

"My pleasure," he muttered.

He eased her up off his lap. She took his hand and led him into the bedroom. He ripped the comforter down on the bed then turned to her, pulling her sweater up and over her head, sliding her bra down and off. He stopped to look at her.

"You're beautiful, incredibly beautiful," he said, staring at her breasts.

She blushed then approached him, pulling at his shirt. She yanked it out of his pants, then unbuttoned it and pushed it off his shoulders. Her eyes widened as they gazed at his chest. A smile played at her lips as she ran her palms up his firm pecs which were covered with fine, light brown hair. She shivered as she touched him, flattening her hands and moving closer to him.

"Not bad, not bad at all," she muttered, looking up at him.

He laughed. "Is that the best you can do?"

"Gorgeous...better?" She asked as she slid her hands up his chest and joined them around his neck, bringing her breasts up against him, pressing closer.

He groaned at the feel of her breasts against him and reached for the button of her jeans. She was unbuttoned and unzipped in a flash, but she had to push the tight pants down herself.

"Drop 'em, handsome," she said to him while she eased her jeans down, watching him get naked.

She stood in her black lace panties, facing him, moving her arms across her chest, feeling suddenly shy. He sucked in his breath at the sight of her and stepped closer, putting his arms around her, slipping his hands down to her butt and pulling her closer to him. He pressed his aching erection against her and a small moan of excitement escaped her lips. She kissed his neck, then his chest.

"You are stunning," he whispered in her ear.

She slid her hands down over his butt and squeezed, then tugged him toward her. Grey slipped his hands under the waistband of her panties and eased them down, cupping his hands over her naked bottom. He groaned into her neck.

She pushed the panties down all the way and stepped out of them. Grey leaned over and trailed his fingers down over her hips to the backs of her thighs, then moved them up and in to lightly caress her core. As they met her wetness, she moaned, opening her thighs to him. His fingers played with her, stroking, circling, slipping inside her a little then out again. She was trembling with desire.

"Oh my God...you...you," she stammered as his fingers continued to caress her; her head fell limp on his shoulder, her eyes closed, she sagged against him. He could feel her pulse leap, heat emanate from her body as she grew slick from the magic his fingers worked on her.

Grey straightened up and led her to the bed. He got on first and then gently pulled her down next to him. He began by kissing her lips then kissing her breasts as his hand, slid across her flat belly and disappeared between her legs. Carrie's legs parted welcoming him. She moaned softly as his fingers explored her warmth.

"Show me where to touch you," he whispered.

"Oh...you're doing fine," she uttered.

"I want to please you, satisfy you. Guide me," he insisted.

He moved his fingers and each time his action received a happy moan from her. It seemed wherever he touched her, she liked it. Then he hit the perfect spot.

"Oh my God! There. There. Just like that," she breathed, arching her back, closing her eyes.

Grey smiled as his fingers brought her pleasure. Irregular breathing didn't stop her from reaching down and wrapping her fingers around his hardness. She stroked him, amazed at how firm he was until she made him groan.

"Stop. Stop," he moaned, placing his hand over hers.

"Why?"

"This will be all over if you don't. I'm...I...oh, God," he moaned into her neck.

Carrie removed her hand and focused on what he was doing to her as her passion escalated, threatening to go out of control. She ached to have him inside her.

"Grey...I...I'm...going...to," she sputtered.

"Come for me, Honey," he whispered in her ear, his fingers disappearing inside her.

His words made it happen as her hips rose in tide with his hand, her muscles clenched and she let out a long groan while the heat of desire filled her body, shooting all the way out to her fingertips and toes.

When her hips relaxed, she felt the fluttering inside subsiding. Panting, she turned to him and kissed his lips softly, gently, putting her palm on his face. His hand came up and wrapped around her breast as he buried his face in her neck.

"Are you protected?"

"On the pill," she whispered back.

"I want to see you...touch you," he breathed as he rolled over on his back and guided her on top of him. She slipped down easily over his erection, burying him deep within her. They groaned together as he disappeared inside her, her warm wetness surrounding him, her muscles squeezing him gently. He pulled her shoulders down to his and attacked her mouth with an aggressive kiss, his tongue taking hers, his hands in her hair. When he let her up, his gaze dropped to her breasts and his hands, too, where they had free access as she moved up and down on him slowly but steadily.

"You're...you're...almost too much...for me," he choked out.

Carrie pushed her chest out toward him and his hands continued to fondle her breasts. She picked up her speed moving on him faster as he moaned louder. Finally, he tucked his arms around her and rolled them both over until he was on top of her. He pumped into her with furious passion, his face buried in her neck, his arms bracing himself as she caught his rhythm and they rocked together. Carrie arched her back as a second orgasm claimed her body. She clutched Grey's shoulders, closed her eyes and let herself go, her hips moving on their own in sync with his, sounds coming automatically from her mouth. As soon as she finished, he signaled his climax with a loud groan, thrusting several more times before relaxing. Carrie felt a fine sheen of sweat coat his back as she ran her fingers down and up his spine.

His eyes closed, his weight bore down on her some though he didn't crush her. The exquisite feeling of skin to skin contact swept through Carrie as her eyes closed. A feeling of happiness washed over her. Thoroughly satisfied, she wound her arms around his neck and kissed his cheek.

"Amazing, Carrie, amazing," he muttered.

She murmured something incoherent and stroked his shoulders. They lay there for a minute or two before he rolled off her and pulled her into his arms, her cheek resting on his chest.

"Happy?" He asked as he palmed her cheek.

"Uh huh."

"Good," he said, closing his eyes, smiling as his hand glided over her back and arms.

They lay in silence for a while. After a half hour, Carrie sat up.

"Coffee and dessert in bed?"

"I'm stuffed, but coffee sounds great," he said, sitting up.

"I can get it," she said, pushing him back down on the bed.

"Not with that bad hand. Let me help," he offered, rising and putting on his boxers.

Carrie threw on a short, silky pink shift and walked ahead of him down to the kitchen.

WHILE CARRIE MADE THE coffee, Grey washed the dishes. She put on some music, picked up a dish towel and dried. Again Michael Bublé's, "Haven't Met You Yet" came on. When Grey finished, he took her by the waist and danced with her, twirling her around the living room to the beat of the song. He pulled her hips close to his and ground them together to the music. She rested her hands on his bare chest as they danced slower, her excitement growing.

When the song was over, she pulled him down for a passionate kiss, while his hands rested on her breasts. Her breath quickened. He backed her up against the wall as the kissing got intense. Grey slipped his hand under her shift and between her legs, his fingers looking for the sweet spot he found earlier. She melted then reached for him, pleased to find him hard already. He quickly worked her into a frenzy, massaging, then slipping his fingers inside her.

"Oh, God...Grey!" She moaned, stroking him.

"Do you want me? He whispered, coming up against her.

"Yes," she groaned.

"Say it, say it, honey, tell me," he murmured, moving his fingers faster.

"I want you...I want you inside me...Take me...*now*," she panted.

He yanked her shift off and picked her up by the waist, setting her on the table.

"Lean back," he ordered.

She leaned her shoulders against the wall while he put a hand under each thigh and pulled her legs up. He dropped his boxers, kicked them off then moved closer to the table, positioned between her thighs and slipped himself inside her.

"Oh my God," she moaned giving herself over to the intense excitement he created inside her as she closed her eyes, resting her forehead on his chest.

With one arm around her shoulders and the other palm down on the table, he thrust into her hard. With every thrust a small sound escaped her lips. He moved one hand to her waist, holding her still as he pounded into her, sweat beading on his forehead and chest. She raised her hands to his hair, then opened her eyes, looking directly into his. His mouth covered hers, his tongue took possession of her mouth.

The pressure inside her grew quickly. He leaned back a little, staring into her eyes with a wicked grin on his face as his fingers stroked her, stimulating her beyond endurance. Her eyes closed as every muscle in her body tightened, held, then released and pure pleasure flooded her veins. When she cracked her eyes open she found him watching.

"You're beautiful when you're..." he started but didn't finish. He grunted and picked up the pace, thrusting harder until he exploded inside her, ending in a long groan.

The silence in the room was broken only by their heavy breathing as the music had finished. She leaned into him with a soft, sweet affectionate kiss.

"You're incredible," she muttered into his mouth.

"You're very...sexy... responsive," he remarked.

"To you...to you...oh baby," she sighed, closing her eyes.

He wound his arms around her and hugged her to him, holding her close. He stroked her hair as her hands slid up and down his back.

Finally he separated from her, retrieved his boxers, then picked up her shift, and helped her put it back on. Grey slipped into the kitchen, returning to the living room with two steaming cups of coffee. They sat on one of the loveseats, put their feet up on the coffee table and watched the dying fire in the fireplace.

Carrie snuggled up and nestled her head into his shoulder. He put his arm around her and sipped his coffee.

"You know everything about me, so let's talk about you," she began.

"Everything? Doubt that." He stroked her hair.

"Maybe not everything, but more than I know about you. If you want to have a family...kids and all how come you're not married? Have you ever been married? You're thirty-four, right?"

"Whoa! One at a time!" He said, putting up his hand.

"You're thirty-four and never been married?" Carrie added more sugar to her coffee.

"Right." His hand rested on her shoulder.

"How come?" She sat up straight and looked directly at him.

"I spent ten years working my ass off, saving every penny, investing to get where I am now,"

"Not an answer."

"Waiting for the right woman to come along," he replied.

"You haven't met her yet?" she said.

"Well..." he blushed and looked away from her, directing his gaze at the fire.

"You haven't met her or you'd be married or at least engaged by now, right?"

"I guess...it's complicated."

"I don't get it, why?"

"Trust me, it is." He directed his gaze out the window, watching a sparrow land on a tree limb.

She shrugged. "When you meet her, you'll know? Then you'll get married?"

"Yeah. What about you? Never married..." He turned back to look at her.

"I didn't say that." She shifted on the sofa, pulling away from him slightly.

"You've been married...and unmarried by the tender age of twenty-nine?"

She nodded.

"Want to tell me about it?" Grey threaded his fingers through hers, his eyes sought hers.

She shook her head. "It's ancient history, was over three years ago." Carrie took a sip of her coffee.

"I get it, it's complicated, right?" A rueful smile played at his lips.

She laughed.

"I don't care about the past. I'm here with you now and that's all that matters to me," he said, drawing her closer, bending down to drop a sweet peck on the tip of her nose.

"Same here. Do you want a bathrobe? It's cold in her," she said, getting up.

"Doubt you have one my size," he chuckled.

"But I do," she said, retrieving two bathrobes from the bedroom. She tossed a blue one to him and put on the pink one.

Grey looked at the robe then looked at her.

"You have so many men sleeping over you bought a robe?"

"And that concerns you, how?"

"Want to know what I'm getting involved in here," he replied, putting on the robe.

"You don't think I'm celibate, do you?"

"Hadn't thought about it."

"I have...needs, just like you. I'll bet you spent ten years sleeping with every female you could get your hands on."

She saw the heat rise in his cheeks.

"That's what I thought. A man doesn't get as experienced as you from reading a book or watching porn!"

"And you?" he asked.

"A woman never tells. I'm not a slut but I have healthy...desires...needs... whatever you want to call it. My past...you said you don't care about the past. It's now with you that counts," she said, slipping her arms around his waist.

"Fair enough," he said, kissing her.

"Good. Let's get some sleep," she said, scattering the smoldering coals in the fireplace, then taking his hand.

"I'm spending the night?"

"You don't want to?"

"Try to kick me out," he said, pulling her to him for a hug and kiss.

She pulled away, turned out the living room lights and led him to the bedroom where she handed him a brand new toothbrush she retrieved from the medicine cabinet.

"These too? You really are prepared for overnight visitors."

She blushed.

"I like my men to be comfortable."

"Honey, if I got any more comfortable, I'd be living here," he murmured in her ear, then kissed her neck.

GREY'S PHONE RANG AND he reluctantly moved away from Carrie to check it. Jenna.

"What' up?" He asked.

"Nothing. Calling to see how your new candidate is measuring up to your list of requirements," she teased.

"Jenna, this is no time for a question like that."

"Is this a baaadddd time?" she said, laughing, "did I catch you...at it?"

"Not exactly." Grey paced, keeping his head down, looking at the floor.

"But you're with her, right?"

"Yes."

"And you can't talk."

"Right." He couldn't keep a note of exasperation from his tone.

"Oh, goody. I have you right where I want you. So, did you get to all *three* items on the list with her yet?" Jenna giggled into the phone.

"I'm not going to answer that question," he said, turning his back to Carrie while he felt heat in his cheeks. "Oh, I see. So you *have*! Well, well, how was it?"

"Jenna!"

"Come on, you can tell me...great, fantastic, terrible? After all, you're the one who asked me if I make my husband beg for sex."

"Bye, Jenna. See you in a few weeks."

"No! Wait! Okay, okay. Just tell me if it's going well. Is it, could she...be...the one?"

"Could be. Gotta go," he said and hung up the phone, anxious to get away from his sister's prying.

"Quite a cryptic phone conversation with your sister...*really* your sister?"

"You don't think that was another woman, do you?"

"Was it?" She cocked her head and planted her feet firmly.

"Absolutely not! Do you want me to call her back so you can speak to her?"

"No, no, I believe you," Carrie said, raising her hands up.

"Good."

"So what were all those one-word answers about?"

"Jenna being nosy, that's all."

"Nosy about what?" Carrie slid onto the bed and sat cross-legged.

Grey hesitated and looked down at his hands, then up into Carrie's eyes.

"About you," he admitted.

"Me? Jenna knows about me? Why? How? Me? Really?" Carrie sat up straight on the bed and coughed twice.

He nodded.

She blushed and clammed up. There was a heavy silence in the room.

"Your family knows about me?" She repeated.

"Should you be a deep, dark secret?"

"I guess not."

"I'm close with my family. We talk...often. Is that a problem? You never talk about men you're dating with your family or friends?"

"I didn't say that."

"Oh...so you *do* talk about men. Do you talk about me?"

She shook her head, then stopped.

"Well, maybe I've mentioned you to my aunt...once or twice and my friend Rosie at the office."

"And I've mentioned you to Jenna. We're even."

"Why?"

Grey stepped closer to her again, pulling her up off the bed and into his arms.

"Because you're special, Carrie," he confessed, closing his eyes.

CARRIE SMILED AT HIM, then disappeared into the bathroom. Grey went in when she came out. He opened the door to find her already in bed and the lights low. He slipped in beside her naked body and curled up behind her, spooning her.

"I checked my phone while you were in the bathroom."

"Any important calls you missed while we were making love?" He whispered, kissing her shoulder.

"A text."

"Oh?" He asked, sitting up and looking at her.

"From Paul Marcel. He wants to publish my book."

"That's fantastic! Congratulations, Carrie," He said, leaning down to kiss her.

"You didn't have anything to do with it, did you?" She asked, rolling over to face him.

"Me? No way. It's business. No matter how much I like you, I can't influence

editorial choices, which books to publish. Those decisions are strictly Paul's. He wouldn't offer a contract unless he thinks the book will sell well...I'm proud of you."

She smiled at him. He resumed his position cuddled up against her. She turned to kiss

him goodnight, then he wrapped his arms around her and they drifted off to sleep.

# Chapter Ten

THEY WERE INSEPARABLE from the first night they slept together. He stayed the next day and they made love three more times. By the next weekend, they had been together three out of five nights. Grey settled his own toothbrush in Carrie's bathroom and she came home from working late to a hot meal, his warm companionship and one of Grey's expert foot massages.

It was a Tuesday, a slow day for Grey. He stopped at Zabar's on the way to Carrie's apartment. A pleasant day, he took his time walking, passing the quirky second-hand, hard-to-find books, Filene's Basement and several small shops plus a deli on his way to 78th Street.

He rounded the corner to her apartment, his arms loaded down with goodies from Zabar's, cold poached salmon, huge cooked gulf shrimp with cocktail sauce, grilled vegetables and a small David's cheesecake for dessert. He climbed the stairs whistling "I Can't Smile Without You", a big grin on his face. When he put the groceries down and put his hand on the knob, the door swung part-way open. Startled, Grey stepped back, dropped his packages and prepared to do battle with an intruder.

When he didn't hear anything, he poked at the door with his finger, standing back alert and ready to have someone lunge at him when a voice came out of the apartment. A female voice.

"Put your hands above your head or I'll shoot!"

Grey did as the voice commanded and stepped slowly over the threshold, his eyes scanning the room. In the corner by the open window facing on the fire escape, poised for a quick exit was an attractive woman in her mid-fifties. She had dark auburn hair in a short stylish hairdo. Artfully applied make-up made her appear about five years younger. She was dressed expensively and in excellent taste, wearing an Armani silk dress in a light chocolate brown print, complimenting her fair complexion. Her long fingernails were painted a dark pink and her high heels were deep brown snakeskin. She held a can of mace trained on Grey. Though her hand shook slightly, she stood firmly rooted to her spot.

"I mean it!" She straightened out her arm, directing the sprayer at his eyes.

"I don't doubt you. I'm terrified. Do I look like a burglar?" Grey tried to keep the smirk off his face.

"Most of the men I know who wear Brooks Brothers don't break into apartments, but you never know," she said, not moving from her spot.

"May I ask who you are?" He asked, lowering his arms until she motioned for him to raise them again waving the can of mace at him.

"I'm Delia Tucker, Carrie's aunt. But the question is who are you?"

"I'm Grey Andrews, her...ah...uh...boyfriend," he said, grimacing at the inadequate word.

"You're her new lover, aren't you?" A slow smile swept over Delia's face.

Grey blushed at the intimate term and nodded. Delia lowered her weapon.

"I guess you're okay," she said, capping the small can of mace and returning it to her Gucci handbag.

Grey returned to the hall to retrieve the bags of food then walked back into the apartment and closed the door. When he turned around, Delia was staring at him.

"Hmmm, Brooks Brothers jacket and pants, maybe L.L. Bean shirt? Gucci loafers, I'd know those anywhere," she said, moving to one of the love seats and sitting down.

"Excuse me a moment," Grey said, retreating to the kitchen to unpack the food and put it away.

Delia sauntered up to the kitchen counter.

"While you're there, do you know how to make a Cosmo?" she asked, lifting her heavily-mascara'd eyelashes up to widen her eyes.

"I do. Does Carrie have the fixin's?"

"Probably not, this cabinet is too small to hold much," Delia said, rummaging through Carrie's liquor supply.

"Can I make you something else?" Grey asked, pulling down two highball glasses.

"It's warm...how about a vodka and tonic. Does she have lime?"

"She does. Bought it yesterday. Vodka and tonic is my poison, too." Grey opened the refrigerator and plucked out a lime.

Delia stepped back to allow Grey access. He pulled out the necessary bottles and cracked some ice from a tray. In five minutes, he handed Delia a frosty glass and motioned her back to the living room.

"Delia... Carrie has mentioned you but hasn't told me much..."

"Maybe that's because you two don't spend much time talking," she smirked.

Grey looked at his drink as warmth crept up his neck.

"Come on...family here. Just teasing! She's told me a lot about you. I'm her aunt, was married to her uncle, the late Jackson Tucker for twenty-two years. I've been a widow for five years." Delia's eyes misted and she directed her gaze out the window.

"I'm sorry."

"I've been in the fashion business all my life. Had a wonderful marriage but never had kids. Now I have Carrie. She may be my niece, but she's more like a daughter to me...especially since her parents are so far away."

"I'm glad she has some family close by..."

"And I want to tell you...if you break her heart...if you mess with her, you mess with me, too," Delia said, her eyes flashed at him.

Grey laughed so hard he almost dropped his drink.

"What makes you think I'm going to break her heart?"

"You're a man, aren't you?" Delia narrowed her eyes.

"Ouch!"

"Maybe that was a tad extreme but I'm very fond of Carrie. She's quite a gal."

"She is. She's amazing!" He took another sip of his drink, keeping his eyes on Delia.

"So why are you here at this hour and what did you bring her?" she asked, crossing her long legs.

"I brought food like I do most nights these days. You're welcome to stay and join us...do you like cold salmon and shrimp?"

"Yum, I certainly do! I saw the Zabar's bag. Do you always bring her food?"

"She's working extra hard on a special project at the agency. I get out early unless I have a deal pending...so I'm feeding her," he explained, finishing his drink.

"Isn't she lucky to have you! I'd love to stay and share dinner, but then I'm off. I have an art gallery opening to attend. I was going to try to take Carrie with me...she's been working too hard. But I'm sure she'd much rather stay here with you."

"Maybe she should go..." he began, trying to be diplomatic.

"Nonsense. She'll have a better time here with you. I hear you give one helluva foot massage," Delia said, opening her eyes fully to stare at him.

Grey covered his embarrassment by rising up to take his glass to the sink.

"Another drink?" he asked her, purposely ignoring her remark.

"There'll be alcohol at the opening. One's enough," she said, downing the rest and leaning over to hand him the glass.

Grey looked at his watch.

"Carrie should be home in half an hour. Just enough time to clean up and get everything set," he said, pulling down some plates from the cabinet and bringing them to Carrie's tiny dining table.

"You really do have dinner ready for her, don't you?"

"Yup."

Delia got up and moved toward the kitchen.

"Let me get the placemats down," she said.

AT EIGHT FIFTEEN, CARRIE turned the knob on her apartment door and walked in to a surprise, seeing her aunt and Grey talking and laughing like old friends.

"I must be going…" Delia said, looking at her Movado watch.

"I thought you were staying. We set the table for three." Grey put his hand on her arm.

"Three's a crowd."

"Stay, Delia. I never get to see you," Carrie said, stealing a glance at Grey.

"Please do. Come on. I mean it." Grey insisted, pulling her back into the apartment by her elbow.

"Well, you twisted my arm," Delia said grinning broadly as she headed for the loveseat. "And there might be time for one more itty bitty drink."

# Chapter Eleven

GREY GOT INTO HIS OFFICE early to go through his mail. He hadn't been working very hard. Tomorrow was November first and they wouldn't be deciding on new ventures until January. So research continued but he could slack off some. His partner, John Whitaker, and John's wife, Renée, always went to the Caribbean for the month of December anyway. Then the first two weeks of January were frantic with Max and Susan presenting their research, John and Grey digesting it all and making decisions on which companies to approach.

But now, now he had time for Carrie. So he enjoyed himself, taking care of her and his spirits soared. He sat back in his chair. Opened his Starbucks coffee and perused the mail piled up on his desk. One envelope he picked up was thick and heavy. An invitation.

He ripped it open to discover his annual invitation to a fund-raising event at the American Museum of Natural History. Grey was on the board of a charitable foundation he started with his three college best friends. They called it The Four Horseman Foundation. Each member had to kick in $100,000 when he became a trustee. Then every year a donation of $20,000 to the foundation was expected. Grey invested the money and each year they paid out $40,000 to various charities. So all the non-profits invited them to their fund-raisers.

The one at the Natural History Museum was his favorite and the only one all four horsemen always attended. He slapped the invitation against his hand, lost in thought. What a perfect place for Carrie to meet his friends without it being formal. He smiled at his plan. Perfect. When Susan came in, he called her into his office.

"I want to RSVP to this invite from the Museum. I know it's after the deadline but..."

"I already did, Mr. Andrews."

"You did?"

"You always go to that event, so I naturally assumed you would this year, too. Since you're been so...uh...preoccupied with other things, I took it upon myself to sign you up...with a guest. I assume you're taking Ms. Tucker?"

"That's the plan. Such foresight should earn you a raise, Susan," Grey commented, chuckling.

"Can I quote you on that?" she retorted, smiling.

Susan left his office and Grey picked up the phone to dial Carrie.

"There's a great party at the Museum of Natural History tomorrow night. It's a fund-raiser they have every year. Do you think you can make it?"

"Tomorrow, Wednesday, huh? Let me see."

There was silence on the phone for a few minutes.

"Is it okay if I don't get there until eight o'clock or so?"

"Sure. Tell me when you can come and I'll send a car for you. You can meet me there."

"Works for me. Let me go and see if I can sweet-talk, Dennis. Later, babe."

Grey pushed back in his chair, put his feet on his desk and stared out the window. *Does life get any better than this?*

GREY WAS WALKING ON air. Carrie hungered for him as much as he did for her, making her mastery of his list complete. He couldn't get enough of her. Waiting so long to find the right woman had been agony and now he had her, he wanted to be with her every night. Evenings during the week, he'd leave work at six to go to her apartment and make dinner, or bring food in. When Carrie returned much later in the evening, he was there to massage her feet, feed her and make love to her. His heart leapt every time the weary expression on her face changed to a warm smile when she opened the door and was greeted by his kiss.

Grey was in love, head over heels in love and planning to take Carrie to the mountains to see the colors change over the weekend with Jenna and Bill in a rented cabin . He picked up his phone and dialed Jenna. He needed to speak with her to confirm their weekend plans and to confide in her his plan for Thanksgiving.

"Jenna, ready for our trip to the mountains?" Grey asked when she picked up the phone.

"Why did you have to wait until it's going to be cold?" Jenna grumbled.

"It will be perfect. Great weather for snuggling...or don't you and Bill do that anymore now that you're married?"

"None of your business! So how's the third item on your list going with Carrie?"

"Do you really want to know, because I'll tell you. Carrie is..."

"That's enough! Stop. TMI, Grey, TMI..."

He laughed into the phone.

"So how is it going? The whole thing with her?" Jenna asked.

"I'm inviting her for Thanksgiving," Grey tossed off.

"What?"

"That's right. She'll be joining us...I hope."

"You've never invited any woman to Thanksgiving before. She must be pretty hot on the third item on the marriage list, eh?"

"I offered to tell you but you didn't want to know..."

"Still don't. You're actually going to bring her to Thanksgiving?"

"That's what I said. Are you losing your hearing?"

"Do mom and dad know?"

"Not yet. I'd better tell 'em slowly..."

"Are you kidding? This will be too good to miss. I wanna be there when you do."

"Then I'm not going to tell you when I'm making the call."

"Aw, come on, Grey."

"Pouting again? I'm immune," he chuckled.

"Didn't used to be."

"I was naïve then. Now I know you do that to get your way. Not working this time. Butt out, Jenna." Grey started pacing in his office.

"Okay, okay. But you'll tell me what they say, right?"

"They'll say, 'how nice, Grey. We'd love to meet her,'" he said, imitating his mother's voice.

"Yeah but you know she'll be dying. The minute you're out of the room she'll probably do a back flip...as will dad. 'it's about time our son settled down'...I can hear him now."

Grey laughed.

"I want to see you tear up your marriage list, Grey, then I want to shop for a dress to wear to your wedding."

"I'm getting there, don't rush me."

"Bill's home. Gotta go."

"Oh? Time for that third item on my list?" He snickered.

"You're impossible. Good bye," Jenna said and hung up the phone.

CARRIE GRABBED HER purse and coat and ran to the elevator. Grey's car would be waiting outside. She got in and called him. The noise of the party in the background made it hard to hear so he walked outside.

"You're in the car?"

"Yes, see you soon."

"Good. The three other Horsemen are here and I want you to meet them."

"Oh, no! The Four Horsemen together?"

"We always meet at this party. I want them to meet you."

"Then I have to change. I'll have the driver stop at my apartment. It won't take me long. I can't meet them looking like this."

"But, Carrie, I'm sure you're..."

She clicked off her phone and leaned forward from the backseat.

"Driver. We have to make one stop before the museum."

She gave him the address then sat back making a mental inventory of what she had to wear that was clean and pressed.

The dark limousine pulled onto the cobblestone drive leading under the giant pink stone arch of the American Museum of Natural History. A rotunda before the arch was filled with perfectly trimmed tiny hedges and clusters of marigolds and zinnias in fall colors of orange and gold.

Grey was pacing out in front of the museum's side entrance on 77th Street when the car drove up. He walked up and opened the door.

"Carrie, I thought I..." then he stopped and simply stared at her.

She wore a fine-gauge cream-colored lined cashmere knit dress. The dress had short sleeves and was low-cut, revealing plenty of cleavage and clung to her like a second skin. Around her neck was a chunky gold link necklace. The matching bracelet clinked with another on her wrist. Small gold hoop earrings were visible when she brushed back her luxurious hair. Burnt orange leather spiked heels brought her closer to Grey's height, though he still had six inches on her. Her lashes, thick with mascara, a touch of blush and coral lipstick were all the cosmetics she needed. A tiny burnt orange clutch bag and a dark, chocolate brown taffeta coat completed the picture. Grey's mouth hung open. Carrie smiled at him and closed the car door.

"Am I late?" She asked, her eyes dancing.

"Oh my God," he muttered when he caught his breath.

"What?" She asked, pretending not to know what he was talking about.

"You look...you look...amazing. Amazing, Carrie."

She gave him a peck on the cheek then folded her arm through his and turned him towards the door. They walked into the large entry way decorated with bronze busts of the founders of the museum. They could hear the far-away laughter and clinking of glasses from an exhibit hall where the party was being held.

"This way to the party?" She asked, following the festive sounds.

He gave a nod and moved forward, his gaze glued to her.

"Amazing," he repeated while she laughed.

THE MUSEUM USUALLY held their parties in the large exhibit hall on the first floor. The exhibits, mostly in glass cases, lined the walls, leaving a long center hall completely free. Food and drink stations at either end allowed people to mingle and wander through the exhibits, chatting, looking at the items on display and replenish their drinks and reload their plates on the other side. Often they show a movie of their progress on new exhibits in their IMAX theater so these big contributors could see where their money is going.

Carrie's heels tapped on the dark marble floor polished to a sheen as she moved toward the food. Draped on Grey's arm, the other three Horsemen couldn't help but notice her. Will, Spence and Bobby were talking together and laughing when Spence spied Grey and Carrie. He stopped talking and stared as Carrie approached, elbowing Will to his right. Will and Bobby turned to see what he was watching.

"Carrie, this is Spence, Will and Bobby...the other three Horsemen. Guys this is Carrie Tucker."

The men muttered greetings as their eyes raked Carrie up and down, giving her the kind of look she was more used to getting in a bar than she would have expected from Grey's friends. She shifted a little, uncomfortably. He pulled her a little closer to him. Spence took Carrie's hand and led her over to the bar.

"Tell me, Carrie. How long have you and Grey been...together?"

"A few months, I think."

"Where have you been hiding her, Grey?" Will asked.

"A few months? Hmmm. You must meet the requirements on the list," Spence said, dropping her hand.

"Grey doesn't see anyone that long who doesn't pass that test..." Bobby said.

"Guys! Guys, hey, give her some breathing room here," Grey said, taking Carrie's hand and pulling her away.

"List?" Carrie asked, her eyebrows raised as she looked at Grey.

"I don't know what he's talking about. Let's get something to eat. I'm starved," Grey said, cupping Carrie's elbow with his hand.

Grey maneuvered Carrie away from the other Horsemen and over to the food table. He introduced her to the head of development for the museum, Lila Samuels.

"Grey told me that you're in advertising? We sure could use some help with our holiday fund-raising promotion. We have bigger goals to reach this year."

"Don't you have an agency?"

"We're a pro bono account, Carrie. Our agencies work for free. Sometimes that works against us. I don't think they always spend enough time on our business."

"I'd be happy to meet you for lunch and brainstorm some ideas."

"That would be fabulous!"

While the women were comparing calendars and making dates, Grey rejoined his buddies.

"Hey, who told you to bring up the list?" he asked Spence.

"Sorry, guy. Doesn't she know about the list?" Spence replied.

"Would you tell a girl about your list?"

"Hell, no. But I've never had a list," Spence said, lifting his wineglass for a sip.

"Maybe you'd be happier if you had," Grey shot back at him.

The smile fell off Spence's face. "You insulting Susan? Wanna step outside and say that again?" Spence said, anger flashing in his eyes.

"I didn't mean anything by it, let's forget it, Spence. You always complain about her. Maybe if you had a list, you'd have everything you want in a woman."

"You're crazy," Spence said turning away from his friend.

"Am I? I have everything I want in Carrie."

The three men stopped in their tracks. Will and Bobby smiled at him.

"It's about time. So when is the big wedding?" Will asked.

"Haven't asked her yet."

"Why not?" Bobby twirled his empty wine glass.

"It's pretty new. Thought I'd wait till the holidays, just to be sure," he said, a blush creeping up his neck.

"No hard feelings, Grey. Didn't know you were that serious," Spence said, extending his hand.

"Yeah, me, too. Susan's great. Keep the list thing to yourselves, guys," Grey said, shaking Spence's hand .

"If you wanted it a deep dark secret, you shouldn't have told Bobby and Spence," Will chuckled.

"Got that right," Grey said, smiling.

"Met your family yet?" Bobby asked, handing the bartender his glass for a refill.

"I'm taking her for a weekend away with Jenna and Bill. Then I thought I'd invite her for Thanksgiving..."

"Thanksgiving? Whoa, that is serious," Will said, raising his eyebrows.

"The holy Andrews Thanksgiving invaded by an outsider. Your parents will flip," Spence said.

"Probably. I need to be sure before I bring her into that lion's den," Grey confided.

"Why don't you wait another ten years, Grey, to be *absolutely* certain? Geesh," Bobby smirked.

"Family...that's the ultimate test. Hell, any woman who looks like her...we like her, right? But your family...Hell, that's different." Spence said.

The guys nodded.

"My mother will be happy she has two arms, two legs and is breathing. It shouldn't be a problem," Grey joked.

"Who's breathing?" Carrie asked, walking up behind Grey.

"You are, honey," Grey remarked, a little color flushing his cheeks. He put his arm around her and hoped she didn't hear any more of the conversation than that.

"What did you say you did for a living, Carrie?" Will asked as he raised his glass to his lips.

Grey let out a sigh of relief as Carrie got involved in a discussion with Will about advertising.

# Chapter Twelve

"IT'S A PERFECT DAY for a drive to the country," Grey said, standing at her window.

"I was lucky to get this weekend off. I'm exhausted," Carrie said, collapsing onto the sofa.

"Come on, pack your stuff, I'm ready to go. The mountain air will be good for you...invigorating!" Grey took her limp hand in his and yanked on it, trying to get her to stand.

"Just let me have a few more minutes like this." She curled up on the sofa and closed her eyes.

"You're going to sleep?"

Carrie opened one eye but didn't move.

"You can sleep in the car, Honey." Grey scooped her up and carried her into the bedroom, placing her on the bed. "A couple of days with fresh air, in the country, with my sister and her husband. Do you good." Grey sat down on the bed next to her, picked up her foot and started massaging it.

"Ummm, that feels good. Don't stop." She rubbed his leg with her other foot.

"If you do that, we'll never get out of here," he chuckled.

"What's your sister like?" Carrie removed her foot from his leg.

"Jenna? I'm closest to her in the family. She's a big tease, so don't believe anything she says."

"What if she says you're terrific?"

"I give you permission to believe that." He reached for her other foot.

"Oooo. I already know."

He leaned over and kissed her.

"What if she doesn't like me?"

"Never happen. She's going to love you."

"How do you know?"

"Because I love you and she's always loved what I loved." He stopped the massage.

"You love me?" Carrie opened her eyes and sat up.

"Of course. Didn't you know?"

She shook her head, "You've never said it before."

"Aren't you supposed to say something here?" He ran his hand through her hair.

"I love you, too. But that went without saying," Carrie tossed off.

"It never goes without saying."

Carrie pulled him down until their lips met in a sweet kiss. When they broke, they stared at each other for a moment before Grey sat up.

"I'll pack." Carrie swung her legs over the side of the bed.

"Right. We can continue this in the cabin." Grey loosened his tie and unbuttoned the top button of his shirt.

CARRIE PICKED OUT CLOTHES and Grey packed them. By 1:30 in the afternoon, they were driving across the George Washington Bridge. The sun was bright and the air cool. Carrie looked out the window and spied leaves changing color on both banks of the Hudson River. Grey steered the XK masterfully over the bridge and onto the Palisades Parkway. The riot of color on the parkway was glorious and though Carrie wanted to sleep, the changing scenes kept her attention. She opened her window, zipped up her blue fleece jacket and settled down in her seat. A sense of contentment washed over her. Expecting to feel afraid and reluctant to meet Grey's beloved sister, instead excitement and good feeling kept her alert. He was right…getting away, a change of scenery and fresh air did invigorate her.

Grey glanced over at her from time to time and smiled.

"So where is this little cabin?" Carrie asked, raising her voice to be heard above the wind whooshing through the small convertible.

"Geneva Heights, about an hour northwest of Pine Grove."

"We're not stopping to see the rest of your family are we?" She sat up straight, panic in her voice.

"It would take me some time and alcohol to prepare you for that."

Carrie breathed a sigh of relief. That would be too serious and she wasn't ready to think about… How could she get serious with him, she didn't even know where her life was going. Keeping the status quo was fine with her. She'd deal with the future when it arrived. She sat back, staring at his handsome profile as he expertly maneuvered the Jag along the winding, leafy parkway.

THE LOG CABIN WAS NESTLED in a small clearing in the woods. A gravel path wound around trees and large shrubs about one hundred feet from the driveway to the house. The key was over the door sill as the realtor promised. Grey carried Carrie's suitcase and his own small bag to the door then opened it.

The musty smell of a closed up house greeted their noses as Carrie ventured in. She looked around, admiring the use of space. There was one great room with a large fireplace serving as living room, dining room and kitchen combined. A sofa and love seat were at right angles in front of the fireplace with a square coffee table between the two. Under the front window of the cabin was the dining room table with six chairs. On the opposite wall was the kitchen. With white appliances and counter space filling the length of one wall and a small oak table with four chairs doubling as kitchen table or work space.

Off the back of the house were two bedrooms. Grey eased by her and went into the far bedroom with light green walls to drop off their bags. Carrie opened windows to let in the fresh air and pulled back curtains to welcome the sunshine. Two doors opened off the kitchen, one to the bathroom and one to the deck behind the house and the outside.

The décor was a charming cross between hunting cabin with plaids in dark green and cream and country sweet with small print bedspreads in lavender and white and matching curtains. Carrie liked it. When she was done, she joined Grey in the bedroom, flopping down backwards on the bed.

"I love it here! This is wonderful, Grey! You were so right."

He looked up from the suitcase he was unpacking and smiled at her, then joined her on the bed. He climbed on, crawling up to her to plant a kiss on her pink lips. Carrie wrapped her arms around him, holding him close.

"When is Jenna coming," Carrie whispered in his ear.

He gave her a wicked grin and replied, "Don't think we have time to make love...they're due soon, but if we close the door..."

"Hello! Hello? Anyone here? Grey?" a feminine voice called out from the front door.

"Too late," Grey muttered as he pushed up from the bed.

Combing his hair with his hands, he walked to the door. Carrie got off the bed and grabbed her purse, searching for a brush. As Grey walked through the bedroom door, Carrie heard a feminine voice.

"Am I interrupting something?" Jenna asked, her eyes twinkling.

"We just got here," Grey said, approaching his sister.

Jenna stepped up to her brother and planted a kiss on his cheek. At that moment, Carrie exited the bedroom, fluffing her hair. She wore a rust-colored scooped-neck long sleeve fine cotton sweater over light blue denims.

Jenna stopped, stared then smiled.

"Wow, you're prettier even than Grey said...I'm Jenna," she said.

Carrie smiled and extended her hand. Jenna brushed her hand aside and gave Carrie a big hug. Jenna wore blue jeans that emphasized her long slim legs but with a dark turquoise sweater that set off her strawberry blonde hair.

"So are you," Carrie remarked when Jenna let her go.

They were interrupted by the arrival of a tall, slim man with dark brown hair, two days' growth of beard and shining dark brown eyes. Carrie walked over to him and extended her hand.

"You must be Bill?"

"You must be Carrie," he replied, taking her hand.

"There's nothing in this house to eat," Jenna announced, after opening and closing cabinet doors and the refrigerator. She threw her jacket on and tossed the car keys to Bill.

"Grocery shopping is on the agenda, I fear," Grey said, tossing Carrie her jacket.

They all piled into Jenna's mini SUV, since Grey's car was too small. Bill drove to the nearest grocery store.

"There's a liquor store, Bill and I'll get some wine. Here, have fun," Grey said, folding a small wad of bills into Carrie's hand before he joined Bill.

Carrie opened her hand and counted out two hundred dollars.

"A bit much for a weekend, isn't it?" She said to no one in particular.

"Grey is generous, always has been," Jenna remarked, slipping her arm through Carrie's and entering the store.

Carrie manned the cart while Jenna shopped. They discussed what to cook and food allergies and dislikes were shared. They picked up the ingredients for lamb stew, one of Grey's favorites, according to Jenna. Carrie volunteered to bake an apple pie. Bacon, eggs, popcorn and other snacks were thrown into the cart along with juice, mixers and beer. In the dairy section, the young women stopped to look over the cheese.

"You'e theperfect match for Grey and the list, too," Jenna said.

"The list? That's the second time I've heard a list mentioned in the past ten days. What is this list?"

Jenna put her hand over her mouth and her cheeks colored.

"Come on, Jenna. You know you want to tell me about the list. What is it? Give!" Carrie wheedled.

"Grey will kill me. It was a slip. Forget it."

"I can't forget it. First Spence, then you..."

"Spence mentioned the list?"

Carrie nodded.

"As long as I'm not the first. I suppose there's nothing wrong with telling you..." Jenna said, justifying her slip of the tongue.

Carrie pulled Jenna over to the bread section where they could be alone and Jenna spilled everything about the list, everything she knew. With every sentence, Carrie's eyes got wider. When the shopping was done, the women filed silently out the door.

"Please don't be mad at me, Carrie..." Jenna pleaded.

"I'm not mad at you, Jenna. I'm grateful you told me."

"I sort of helped though."

"I need to straighten this out with Grey," Carrie said, sticking her chin out a bit and clenching her jaw.

The men tried to start conversation in the car but the ladies were unresponsive. Carrie kept her eyes trained on the road, refusing to look at Grey. Bill and Grey exchanged puzzled looks and finally sat silently until pulling into the driveway of the cabin.

Grey took two bags in then pulled Carrie aside, took her into the bedroom and closed the door.

"What's going on?" he asked, his hand clamped around her upper arm.

"You tell me. Tell me about your list," she said, standing with legs apart, hands on her hips.

Grey turned pale and dropped his hand.

"So it's true. You have a list of qualities...or should I say *qualifications* for a wife?"

"Sort of..." he stammered.

"And I meet these requirements?"

"You do."

"So now...I'm 'it'?"

"It's not like that, Carrie. You're different..."

"How so? If I hadn't met all those...things...would you still be seeing me?" She asked, watching him squirm.

"Maybe...maybe not. But you do and you're spectacular...way above and beyond..."

"Bullshit, Grey!" She hollered.

Grey gave a quick glance at the closed bedroom door.

"Let's go for a walk. We can talk in the woods where it's more private. How did you find out about the list?" He asked, moving toward the door.

"Jenna told me." Carrie stated flatly.

Grey opened the door.

"Jenna!" He yelled, his face turning purple.

Jenna saw his face and ran out the front door. Bill put down the groceries he was unpacking and followed his wife.

"It isn't her fault...it's yours!" Carrie pulled Grey by his sleeve toward the back door.

They walked in silence through the woods to a pond. Carrie found a large rock jutting out of the earth and sat down, pulling her knees to her chest.

"I don't know what's wrong with having a list of the qualities you're looking for in a mate, Carrie. Women do the same...or so Jenna told me. Why are you upset?" He sat down on the rock next to her.

Carrie shot him a withering look.

"Explain it to me, honey." He stroked her arm.

She yanked herself away from him and stared out at the pond.

"Do you think I'm some sort of Stepford Wife, one who will cook for you, decorate your house and give you all the sex you want at the drop of a hat?"

"I don't, I don't think of you that way."

"Then how do you think of me?" Tears stung at the back of Carrie's eyes but she was determined to blink them away.

"I think of you as my ideal woman, smart, creative, resourceful, sexy...the woman I love," he said, slowly, quietly.

"That stupid list! Everyone knows about it...everyone but me! Jenna wouldn't explain the third item on the list, said she didn't know exactly what it was but it had something to do with getting enough sex and then she blushed redder than the beets on display in the produce department."

Grey laughed.

"What's so funny?" Carrie sniffed.

"You are. Do you care that my friends and...Jenna...know about my list? Don't you think it's a miracle I found a woman I'm crazy about that also has those qualities?"

"I think it's a miracle I haven't killed you yet..." She sniffed, turning away from his warm stare.

"I admit those things are important to me, because...because...well the other three Horsemen complain about their wives lacking those things. So I thought, if I could get those in a mate, then I'd be a lot happier than they are."

"Now finding a spouse...the best spouse is a four horseman competition?"

"It's more about me than about them. I want to get married once and have it last forever. I'm picky...okay, maybe fussy is a better word...but look at you...and how lucky I am?"

With his last words he bent down and kissed her. Carrie tried to remain angry but couldn't. His kiss stole her anger away.

"Stop that," she said, pushing him away. "You're trying to make me forget."

"Am I? I thought I was enjoying kissing my girl," he whispered.

"This is how you made your money, isn't it? Sweet talk, charming people into getting your own way."

"If I had my way, we'd be back in our bedroom in the cabin doing something completely different than arguing about a dumb list." His eyes made contact with hers while his hand touched hers tentatively.

"So what exactly was that third item on your list," she asked, casting her gaze at the rock for a second before looking into his eyes. She linked her pinky with his.

"Sure you want to know?"

"I asked, didn't I?" she said, turning angry eyes on him.

Grey shifted his weight and cleared his throat before he explained the third item on the list. Carrie stared at him in disbelief, then she burst out laughing.

"I can't believe you've basically told all your friends and family how I feel about sex...that I'm as horny as a man. And then you sit there telling me I'm foolish to be embarrassed!"

"Oh, I thought you were really laughing there, for a minute. Actually it is funny if you look at it from a different perspective..."

"From what perspective? I can't face the other three Horsemen and your sister...your sister who was too embarrassed to even make reference to it...and her husband who probably knows all about it..." Tears spilled over and streamed down cheeks flushed with humiliation.

"What's wrong with being sexy?" Grey said, taking her in his arms.

"It's private. What goes on between you and me is private," she stated.

She gave him token resistance but stopped when he wouldn't let her go. Carrie loved being in his arms. She felt safe, loved and protected. She closed her eyes and let those feelings wash over her again.

"Let them all be jealous that we are so...so...compatible," he chuckled.

"Compatible! You've told them I want sex all the time! Which isn't true, by the way," she said, then turned her face into his chest.

"I never told anyone that...or mentioned anything we do together. I've never spoken of you that way and I wouldn't," he insisted.

She burrowed her face into his shoulder while her breathing returned to normal.

"Let's not let this ruin our weekend, Carrie. We're here in this great cabin with Jenna...and I could tell you plenty of embarrassing things about her...and Bill, too. I just might if they give you a hard time. Let's be together and be in love, honey," he said, stroking her hair.

Carrie was seduced by him as always. His soothing manner, his sense of humor and his sexy, hard body coupled with his desire for her...she found him irresistible. When she moved back and looked up at him, his mouth came down to cover hers in a passionate kiss.

"I'll try," she said, wiping her cheek with her fingers.

Grey pulled a handkerchief out of his pocket and dried her tears. He pushed off the rock to his feet then offered his hand to Carrie. She took it allowing him to pull her up. They turned to find their way back to the cabin, Grey with his arm around her shoulders and Carrie with her arm around his waist.

They arrived at the cabin to find Jenna and Bill had put out some cheese and crackers and opened a bottle of wine. A small fire was getting started in the fireplace. They turned and looked at Carrie and Grey as they walked in the back door. Jenna's eyes didn't meet Grey's. Grey took a piece of paper out of his pocket, wrote something on it and walked over to the fireplace.

"Here it is, The List," he said.

Then he ripped it into pieces and tossed it into the fire.

"And I forbid anyone in this room from ever mentioning it again."

Bill poured two more glasses of wine and handed one to Carrie and one to Grey. Then he raised his glass in a toast. Jenna joined him.

"I'll drink to that," Bill said, taking a healthy sip of his wine.

# Chapter Thirteen

"WHEN YOUR WORK SCHEDULE calms down, maybe you can come up to my place for a night," he said, closing the screen on her fireplace and standing up.

The fire he laid jumped to life as flames shot up and the small logs began to catch. He watched it and grinned in satisfaction as he sat down on the sofa. Carrie put down her glass of cabernet sauvignon and settled her right foot in his lap. Grey took another sip, returned the glass to the coffee table and began to massage Carrie's foot. She closed her eyes and sank down into the sofa resting her head on a red print pillow leaning against the arm.

"Tough day?"

"Hmm," she said with a nod, "but we always talk about me. How about your day?"

"A drag. I spend the whole day going over figures for a new company, a solar farm. It was boring as hell."

"Are you going to invest in the farm?" She asked, a small sigh of pleasure slipping out of her mouth as he kneaded under the ball of her foot.

"I don't know yet. Farms are risky but if this one could exist only on solar power, it might work."

Carrie picked up her right foot and moved her left foot into his lap.

"Do you have plans for Thanksgiving?" He tried to keep his voice nonchalant.

"Thanksgiving?" she asked, her tone weary.

"You know, the holiday that comes every year...the third Thursday in November?" He teased.

She shot him a dirty look.

"I'm not brain-dead...not yet, anyway. I usually spend it with my aunt Delia and whatever boyfriend is the flavor of the month," she said.

"Do you think she'd mind if you spent it with me and my family?" He kept his tone even, but his pulse was racing, listening for her response.

Carrie sat up and raised an eyebrow.

"Didn't Jenna say something about Thanksgiving being a special holiday at your house?"

"All holidays are special with my family..." he began.

"No, no, I specifically remember her saying Thanksgiving."

"Well...sort of, maybe. Might be. But it's just the family."

"This year you want it to be just the family and me?"

"I'd like that." His hand stopped rubbing and closed around her small foot.

"Delia's not the overly sentimental type...I doubt she'd miss me that much and she definitely likes you...hmm," Carrie stroked a pretend beard on her chin.

"So that means you'll come," he asked, eyebrows raised.

"If you want me to, sure," Carrie said, grinning at him.

"Great! You're coming!" Grey dropped her foot to the side and pushed up off the sofa, rushing eagerly to the balcony to make a call.

He kept his voice low as he spoke to his mother and watched Carrie sink into the sofa and close her eyes.

"So we're finally going to meet this mystery woman of yours, eh?" His mother remarked.

"Looks that way. She's coming for Thanksgiving..."

"Thanksgiving!"

"Yes."

"John! John! Grey's bringing his girl out for Thanksgiving!" Grey heard his mother speaking to his father on the side.

"Gotta go, Mom."

"Wonderful, dear. We're so happy she's coming then."

"Nothing out of the ordinary, okay?" he asked with a tinge of worry in his voice.

"I don't know what you're talking about."

Grey laughed. "All right. I'll be ready for anything." He said, running his hand through his hair.

He heard his mother chuckle before she hung up the phone and for a second he wondered if this was the right move. Hell, what did he know about the right move? He'd never gotten this close to a woman before and the confident businessman realized he was navigating uncharted waters...completely out of his element.

By the time he got back to the sofa, Carrie was fast asleep. He picked her up and carried her into the bedroom. Undressing her was a treat for him though it didn't appear he'd get to do much more than enjoy looking at her. She tossed and stretched but didn't seem to come fully awake. He took off his clothes, too, and joined her in the bed.

He switched off the light and turned on his side, slipping his arm over Carrie's naked body and pulling her in close to him. She sighed and placed her hand over his. He buried his face in her neck breathing in the faint scent of her lilac perfume still lingering there and the sweet smell of her skin. He didn't know what he was supposed to do next. He was flying blind, letting love lead the way.

His mind wandered to Thanksgiving upstate with his family and Carrie. He shuddered slightly to think of how many references to marriage his mother would make in Carrie's presence, or how his older sister Barbara would trot out every baby picture she could find of him, especially the most embarrassing ones. But then there was Jenna. Surely she would make Carrie feel more comfortable. Grey closed his eyes. He hoped all would go well. This would be the first test...no actually finding out about the list was the first test. This was the second. Poor Carrie. He hoped their love would survive a day with his family as he drifted off to sleep.

CARRIE AWOKE AT THREE a.m. to go to the bathroom. Feeling wide awake, she slipped on a robe because the apartment felt cool, and padded into the living room. She perched by the window to watch the moon. It wasn't a full moon but only half. Still it shone down on the sleeping City with a silvery white glow. The moonlight on the bare branches of the trees shaded them, emphasizing their roundness. It created creepy shadows that could be providing hiding places for thieves or lovers with nowhere else to go.

The chill in the apartment penetrated her thin silk robe so she returned to the warmth of her bed. Grey was asleep, on his stomach with his arms up around his head. She slipped in quietly, trying not to jostle the bed and wake him up but he rolled over on his side anyway, the covers sliding down to his waist. Lying on her back, Carrie gazed at his face and his chest in the dim light from streetlights filtering in her window. His face appeared relaxed and boyish with his hair mussed by sleep, except for the slight growth of beard on his cheeks belying his age. *How handsome he is.* His strong chest had a light coating of sandy colored hair. The feel of it called to her and she reached out, flattening her hand against him slowly. He barely moved. She ran her hand ran up and then down his chest as she enjoyed the feel of his skin and muscle beneath her fingers. A small sigh escaped her lips.

Grey slung his arm around her, his hand on her back as she faced him. Carrie rolled over, her back to him, fitting herself into the curves of his body, snuggling up against him.

A few unintelligible sounds escaped from his throat as she took his hand and pulled his arm around her, resting his hand on her belly. Grey splayed his fingers against her skin and pulled her up tight against him.

"Cold," he muttered.

"Not anymore," she whispered, feeling the heat from his body penetrate hers.

Grey moved his hand up slowly across her ribcage to rest on her breast. A small shiver raced up her spine.

"Still cold?" he asked, now awake.

"Not cold..."

"More?"

He closed his fingers around her breast and began a gentle massage. She closed her eyes and let his hand work its magic on her body. His lips caressed her neck with small kisses, sending another shiver up her spine. He chuckled.

'You're a magician," she whispered.

"Am I?"

His fingers gently tweaked her peak, sending signals down to her core. She squirmed, wiggling her bottom up against him and felt his growing arousal.

"You touch me in one place and I feel it in another."

He laughed softly. Then he glided his hand slowly down her smooth skin to her thigh.

'You feel soooo good," he whispered.

Carrie rolled over on her back and placed her hand on his shoulder. He slid his fingers to her inner thigh as she parted her legs for him. Burying her face in his neck, she opened her mouth and sucked on his skin gently, caressing it with her tongue, eliciting a moan from him.

His fingers moved to up into her core. She groaned and hooked her leg over his hip as heat shot through her body.

"Oh, God," she moaned, removing her lips from his skin and throwing her head back against the pillow. In the dim light she could still see his eyes, staring straight into hers. Her breath came quickly as desire claimed her.

"I want you," she muttered, her eyes never leaving his.

She reached down, curling her fingers around his erection. "Oh, my."

He laughed.

"I guess you want me, too."

"Could say that," he agreed as he brought his hand around to the back of her thigh and moved it up to her butt.

"Ready?"

"Been ready..."

Grey chuckled.

Carrie lifted her leg higher, folding it against his body as his hand pulled her close enough for him to slide into her. She gasped as he entered her, closing her eyes again, focusing on the wonderful feeling of him inside her.

"Ohhhh...honey," he moaned, holding her tightly against him.

He started to move in and out of her, slowly at first.

"Oh, God...Grey..." she groaned.

As she got more excited, he moved faster. Carrie managed to move her hips with him only slightly as his grip was tight. Still, pleasure coursed through her veins, growing with every thrust. As the intensity grew, she panted and her grip on his shoulder tightened. As the excitement spiraled up, her climax exploded, tensing every muscle and nerve before releasing bliss all the way down to her toes. Carrie emitted a stifled cry. Grey pushed harder. But that didn't last long as he let out a long groan signaling his release.

They laid in each others arms. Carrie reached up to touch Grey's cheek and felt the dampness on his forehead. He kissed her lightly, his hand brushing back her hair.

"You beat an alarm clock...hands down."

She laughed. "I bet you say that to all the girls."

"Never had one wake me up in the middle of the night to make love before."

"Really?"

"Really. Fantastic," He kissed her again, then pulled up the sheet and blanket, draping it over her body to protect her from the cold air in the bedroom.

"That wasn't my intention. I couldn't sleep but when I saw you lying there so peacefully...I...I...got turned on."

"Music to my ears. You can wake me up that way anytime, Honey."

"Feeling sleepy now," she admitted, yawning.

They cuddled together in spooning position.

"Sweet dreams, Carrie."

"You, too, Grey."

# Chapter Fourteen

PRESSURE CONTINUED to mount during the next weeks at her job. Late night after late night, corrections, constant revisions, whole campaigns were scuttled only to be begun again. She was exhausted, frazzled but also wildly in love. Carrie never met anyone like Grey and the more her work life deteriorated, the more she craved his company.

Carrie hustled in early on the Wednesday before Thanksgiving to see Mr. Goodhue, the president of the agency, who wanted to meet with her at eight o'clock. She was nervous because he never wasted time with unimportant meetings or unimportant people. He had a staff to take care of trivia, so if he wanted to see her, it must be important.

She came into his office quietly. He looked up at her, nodded and motioned her to sit down.

"Coffee?"

"Thanks," she said, raising her cup to show him she brought her own.

"Carrie, I have watched your progress for three years now and have been very pleased to see you blossom from the shy, unhappy young woman who started here to a confident, accomplished writer. Your work on the new business team is excellent. I think the next piece of business we bring in that you spear-headed might be your promotion to creative director."

She smiled at him, pleased at the praise, but noticed he did not smile back. Her stomach sank and her heart rate increased. Somehow this didn't feel good.

"You're well liked, too. Rosie has been singing your praises on working with the production department...and..." he continued.

"Mr. Goodhue, this sounds like either a eulogy or obituary. Which is it and why am I dead?"

"We're in a difficult situation with Country Lane Cosmetics," he said, putting up his palm when she tried to speak.

"I know the account is in jeopardy. This is a different kind of jeopardy. You know Country Lane got a new president, one who has his own favorite ad agency he's worked with for years, right?'

"I've been killing myself working on the pitch to keep the business."

"You know how many people are involved in this business, here at the agency, right? How many people would have to be let go if we lost Country Lane?"

"Plenty."

"Do you know someone named Grey Andrews?" He asked her, picking up his mug for a sip of coffee.

She gulped and felt her face get hot. Her eyebrows shot up.

"Grey? Why do you ask?"

"How well do you know him?"

"Well enough, what does that have to do with..."

"Are you sleeping with him, Carrie?" Nathan put down his coffee cup and stared hard at her.

Her face got redder when anger combined with embarrassment.

"That's my private business, Nathan..." she sputtered.

"Not when his sister is the new ad director at Country Lane, it isn't."

"What?"

"So are you...on intimate terms with him?"

"I'm in love with him."

"Oh, boy," he said, looking down at his thumbs, "this is going to be harder than I thought."

"I don't see the problem. What does Grey have to do with anything?"

"The new president is pushing to have us fired. Barbara Andrews likes the work we have done. But she told me at breakfast yesterday you're involved with her brother. It could be construed as undue influence if she evaluates us and recommends Country Lane keep us as their agency. If that information leaks out to her boss, she'll get fired for showing favoritism. She wants to make a fair decision, one she can support to her boss, but if he finds out about you and this guy..."

"Grey?"

"Then her judgment is compromised. Who wouldn't think she'd want to keep her future sister-in-law employed? It's practically nepotism. She might have to fire us, simply to appear impartial. Either way, it doesn't look good for us...," he paused, "as long as you are here."

"And if I stop seeing Grey?"

"That might work...personally, I think it's too late for that."

"Good, because I wouldn't."

"I didn't think so. You have integrity, Carrie, one of the things I've always liked about you..."

"Stop buttering me up, Nathan," she said, suddenly unafraid to be direct, "you want me to quit, right?"

"I'd put you on another piece of business, though I'm not sure that would be enough except we don't have another piece of business for you."

"So I'm going to get the shaft here, right?" She felt tears at the backs of her eyes but would be damned if she'd let him see her cry. She took a deep breath, blinked a few times and got her emotions under control.

"Well...there are so many people involved here, production, traffic, account services, not to mention your own creative team...say ten people in all who would lose their jobs if you stay here and continue to see Barbara's brother. What do you think is the fair thing to do here?"

Tears pricked her eyes. Choose, Grey or her job?

"I'd make it easier and fire you but that wouldn't make things better. We would look bad, all of us. And I don't want it on your record. Your work is excellent and you haven't done anything wrong. Perhaps if you stopped seeing him, I could talk to Barbara and your job could be saved. This is not a great time to be out of work, especially in our business. It's your call."

She nodded, emotion choking her so her throat closed up. She worked so hard to make a success here. After her marriage blew apart, she was destroyed. GWB had become her home after her divorce, a place she felt she belonged. And she had been rewarded for her hard work and loyalty with regular raises and a promotion. The agency took her in, gave her a job and nurtured her, helped her, taught her and appreciated her work. Now, in the blink of an eye, it might all be over.

"Barbara wasn't mad at you, hell, she hasn't even met you, she told me, although she admitted she's heard about you from her other sister. She was insistent we take action. I assured her I would speak with you privately and you would make a decision in the best interest of everyone," he said, standing up to indicate their meeting was over.

"I'll have my letter of resignation on your desk by ten o'clock. Do you mind if I leave afterward?"

"Why don't you think it over during the holiday? There's plenty of time to resign on Monday, when you get back, if that's what you want. I'd be heartbroken to lose you, but applaud your selflessness in putting your colleagues first. You can count on me for a glowing recommendation to your next employer...if you choose him over us," he said, shaking her hand.

Carrie was numb. She went into her office and printed out the letter, before the tears started. Then she ripped it up and threw it in the trash. She closed her door, packed up and walked toward the hall. On the way out, she passed Dennis.

"Where are you going?" He asked, reaching for her arm.

She yanked her arm away from him and kept walking, refusing to respond to his repeated calls to her.

On the street, she looked for a coffee shop and found a Starbucks two blocks away. She went in and ordered her usual Latte and sat down. Tears flowed down her cheeks as she hid her face. All that time wasted and the new campaign, the new business pitches, the late nights, the stress...all for nothing. What did she have now? No job, no salary...nothing. Not nothing. She had Grey.

But did she? How long had she known him? A few months. What if his family didn't like her? She didn't have any guarantee of a future with Grey. He wouldn't be the first man to take a powder on her in her life. Instead of feeling more secure about Grey, she felt less. *That's not fair. He hasn't done anything wrong. But I still don't feel like I can rely on him to be there for me. Marriage? We haven't discussed it since that day we fought about the list.* Feeling a familiar throbbing at her temples, she massaged her head with her fingertips then popped two ibuprofen to head off the approaching headache.

Tomorrow she would meet his family for Thanksgiving. Stay in their house. In the same room with Grey. Oh, God! His sister, the ad director for Country Lane would be there. The woman responsible for putting her in this predicament! No way was she going there.

Carrie finished her coffee and hit the street. It was only one o'clock but traffic was piling up. People had begun their holiday journeys and the City would be a tangle of sports cars, SUVs, taxis, busses and trucks all vying for space and honking their horns until they were hoarse. The trip back to her apartment was arduous as streets were closed due to the Macy's Thanksgiving Day Parade backing up traffic for block after block.

Her street and several other side streets were cordoned off. Some people had figured out it was better to come watch the balloons being blown up the day before than to be there on parade day. So they flooded the site like flocks of migrating Canada geese, honking and elbowing everyone out of the way. Parents with strollers and toddlers in tow, teens, even grandparents came down to see the balloons. Then they could stay in the comfort of their own homes on the holiday and watch football on TV.

Carrie walked to the bus which inched along, missing every green light, making her feel trapped in its stuffy atmosphere with people talking loudly on cell phones or sneezing in her face. She called her Aunt Delia.

"Hey, Delia, can you squeeze in another place tomorrow?" She asked trying to steady her voice.

"You're coming? What's wrong?" Delia asked.

"Nothing. Can't I change my mind and prefer to be with you?"

"Hah! I'm not fooled. Last time I saw you, you had stars in your eyes, now you can hardly keep from crying. I hear it, Carrie, I hear it in your voice."

"I'm on the bus and can't talk."

"You pack up and get your little fanny on the four o'clock train this afternoon. I'm chilling your favorite, Moscato and pulling out another wine glass. You come up here and tell me all about it."

"Who all is coming tomorrow?"

"Tony and his son, Marco. Freddie and her husband, Harold. Sam Wood and Joanie Johnson."

"Small crowd...hey you're having Sam and Tony together?"

"Yeah. Sam is last year's flavor and Tony is this year. Sam won't mind. He's got a new lady but she's out of town."

Carrie laughed in spite of her predicament. "I'll be there."

"Okay, Cookie, see you then."

Carrie hung up the phone just as the bus reached Amsterdam Avenue. She got off the bus and walked a block to her building. Grey! Oh, God. She's had to call him. After packing her suitcase and drinking half a glass of wine to steady her nerves, she picked up her phone.

"Hi, beautiful! Are you still at work?" He asked.

"I'm home..."

"I can come over for some alone time...if you're interested."

"Not tonight, there's a problem..." Carrie's voice cracked.

"What? Something wrong?"

"I can't go with you tomorrow," she said and held her breath.

"Why?" His voice rose an octave.

"Something happened today at work...and I'm...I've got to make a decision. About my job...and about you. So I'm going to Delia's because I need to think."

"Think...at Delia's? A decision? What kind of decision?" His voice sounded tight.

"I don't want to discuss it on the phone," she demurred, hoping he'd leave it at that but certain he wouldn't.

"Then I'll be right over," he countered.

"You can't get here. The streets are clogged from one river to the other. The parade, remember?"

"I don't care. I'll walk then."

"Grey, I don't want to talk to you right now."

"Why not?"

"Ask your sister, Barbara, about it when you see her tomorrow."

"Barbara? What's she got to do with us?"

"Everything. Train leaves in an hour and it will take me that long to get to Grand Central. I've gotta go," Carrie said, hanging up the phone.

She burst into tears and sank down on the sofa. The phone started ringing, it was Grey and she let it ring. Then he hung up. And called back. And hung up. And called back. *He's persistent, I'll give him that.*

Carrie whipped out the hard copy of her mystery book manuscript stuffed the pages into her briefcase with her computer. She'd begin working on the edits she received from Paul Marcel at Delia's. An ironic smile crossed her lips. *Looks like I could get my wish to be a fiction writer after all, an unemployed fiction writer.*

She slung her bag over her shoulder, tucked her purse into her briefcase and secured that under her arm. She left the phone ringing and trudged down the stairs then down the street to the subway, the only method of transportation in the City that would not have ground to a halt because of the parade.

THE WEATHER STARTED to deteriorate; the sun disappeared behind light gray clouds. Carrie opened her computer and tried to focus on her edits for the hour and a half ride to Shelton, Connecticut. But all she could do was look out the window, dream and think about what she wanted. When the train screeched to a halt, it's wheels screaming, Delia Tucker was standing next to her White Toyota Rav, waving. Carrie smiled to see her beloved aunt and felt better.

Delia enveloped the young woman in her arms Carrie immediately burst into tears. They stood there for a minute until Carrie could control herself. Delia picked up the bag and tossed it in the backseat while Carrie climbed in the front.

"Where are you parents?" Delia asked while she pulled out of the parking lot.

"Traveling. I think it's Thanksgiving in Turkey this year," she laughed, "That's ironic!"

"Still traveling?"

"A Mediterranean cruise, I think. They never took vacations when I was a kid. Work, work, work..."

"That's where you get your work ethic."

"I suppose. They're entitled to live the way they want now. It might be nice if they made more time for you."

"I'm used to it. It's okay."

Delia changed the subject and they chatted about the preparations for the next day on the ride home, skirting the one issue that was gnawing at Carrie until they were ensconced in Delia's kitchen, each with a glass of cool Moscato wine and some cheese and crackers in front of them.

"Apple pie or pumpkin...or both?" Carrie asked, rolling up her sleeves.

"I think I have the ingredients for both," Delia said, perching on a high stool.

Carrie pulled out the flour, butter and salt. Then she took a large bowl, a couple of knives and a rolling pin.

"This new granite countertop is perfect to roll dough on."

"Knock yourself out. So while you're rolling pie dough, tell me what's going on." Delia refilled Carrie's glass then sat back.

Carrie recounted her conversation with Nathan Goodhue and her dilemma.

"What do you want to do?"

"I don't know for sure...I've worked so hard and am so close to becoming a creative director...but Grey is so amazing..."

"Seems to me that Goodhue didn't give you much choice. Don't you have to resign?"

"Not exactly. If I gave up Grey, then I could stay. But I don't want to give him up."

"Ah, I see. The old I want my cake and eat it too dilemma. Hmmm. That's not going to work here, Cookie."

No one had called her "Cookie" in a long time. Delia was the first to nickname her that and her parents liked it, so it stuck. As the air got colder outside, Carrie turned on the oven to preheat. She was enjoying being in the warm kitchen in Delia's company.

"What do you really want out of life, Carrie?"

"Why don't you ask me something really big, Delia?" She laughed.

"Seriously. Do you want to be a creative director? Do you want to marry Grey..."

"Hold on! He hasn't asked me or anything."

"Going to his family's house for Thanksgiving? You don't think that's a prelude to a proposal?" Delia raised her eyebrows and took a sip of her wine.

Color came to Carrie's cheeks.

"I didn't want to see it that way."

"How does he feel about you standing him up?"

"Not too good, I'd guess," Carrie said, frowning.

"Did you tell him what happened?"

Carrie gave her head a shake.

"I didn't want to see him. I didn't want to tell him over the phone. He would have tried to talk me into going with him anyway and his sister's going to be there and..."

"So you bailed without an explanation?"

"I guess I did."

"Not good, Cookie."

"I told him to ask his sister, Barbara. He asked me what that meant and I sort of hung up on him."

"You didn't! Oh, Cookie! Grey is...he's...a keeper, a real keeper." Delia clucked her tongue at Carrie.

Carrie took down the pie pan, avoiding Delia's eyes.

"Do you love him?" Delia asked, softly leaning toward her niece.

Carrie stopped what she was doing and gave a slight nod with her head as two tears escaped down her cheeks.

"What if it doesn't work out? My track record isn't good. Grey has never had a serious relationship...what if he leaves me? Then I have nothing." Carrie began to pace the length of the kitchen and chew her lip.

"What if you get fired for another reason? There are no guarantees on either side of this dilemma," Delia said, sitting back again and finishing the wine in her glass.

"Then what do I do?"

"I can't tell you what to do. Listen to your heart. Underneath all that intelligence, your heart knows what's going on and what the right move is."

Carrie put the pie in the oven as the phone rang. It was Tony, and Delia disappeared into her bedroom, closing the door. Carrie went over to sofa in front of the fireplace where a small fire burned slowly, and sat down. The smells of the room in her aunt's wonderful house soothed her. She had spent many happy days here in this little stone house. Memories of sleepovers at Aunt Delia and Uncle Jack's house, shopping trips with the savvy Delia, and Uncle Jack teaching her to bake bread came flooding back, warming her heart.

She missed Uncle Jack, missed being a kid again where her biggest decision was whether she should have chocolate ice cream or strawberry for dessert. She hugged her knees to her chest and thought about Grey. What if he didn't disappear? What if Delia was right and this schlepping her to meet his family was a prelude to a marriage proposal? Would she want to marry him? *Get back into that saddle again? Leave my career behind after all the sweat and tears? If the marriage doesn't work, where will I be? If there is no marriage, where will I be? An unemployed fiction writer.* Carrie hadn't been in love since her divorce. Her ex-husband moved to the West Coast, telling her he was too young for such a commitment. The responsibility and restrictions of marriage had weighed too heavily on Todd. He wanted his freedom, he wanted out and he broke her heart. Now, three years later, would Grey do the same thing? Was he "a keeper" like Delia said? Too many questions and too few answers.

As Carrie watched the fire burn down, Delia finished her phone call and returned to the living room. She sank down next to Carrie on the sofa.

"So, did you find the answer you're looking for?"

Carrie continued to stare at the fire and shook her head.

"It's like a game of *Chutes and Ladders*, Delia. I'm at the mid point, one step and either I will take a ladder up, or a chute down to the beginning again." Carrie stood up and returned to the kitchen to check on her pie.

GREY BROKE WITH TRADITION, got in his car and drove north to Pine Grove on Wednesday night. Usually he'd leave at seven a.m. on Thanksgiving Day arriving in time for breakfast. It was tradition for his whole family to gather for a big breakfast made by his dad and then not to eat again until the big meal. After breakfast everyone pitched in. They had assigned tasks and worked side-by-side, laughing, joking and teasing while they straightened the house gathered firewood, sliced, chopped, rolled, basted and tossed everything for the huge dinner. Most of his siblings arrived the night before. Grey hated driving through the bumper-to-bumper traffic slowly leaking out of Manhattan on Wednesday night. So he arose at the crack of dawn and had an easy drive up the Palisades and Route 17.

But tonight he was too agitated to stay in his house. He paced and paced until he couldn't stand it anymore. Barbara would be there tonight and he had to find out what was going on. By seven o'clock he couldn't stand it anymore, so he threw his bag in the trunk. The Jag roared to life and headed north. On his way to the Palisades he was surprised to find a donut hole in the traffic and he had little difficulty until he reached the George Washington Bridge, where traffic came to a halt.

Feeling his temper rising, he turned on the radio, flipping the dial to find some calming music when he came upon Michael Bublé's song, "Haven't Met You Yet". He stopped surfing, sat back and listened, remembering the first night they made love. As he inched across the bridge through the dark of early evening, he smiled when he recalled dancing with Carrie, then taking her on the table. How beautiful she was when he was making love to her; lost in passion, the fire in her eyes, her body soft and pliable, bending to him, responding to his every touch. He began to get hard losing himself in the memory. The feel of her skin, the taste of her lips, the fullness of her breasts wouldn't leave his mind.

*I'm not giving up!* When the song finished, he surfed until he found a classical music station. The music calmed him and allowed him to think on the way to Pine Grove. By the time he reached exit 12 the traffic had thinned out. He drove most of the rest of the way on automatic pilot, focusing on Carrie and their time together.

*I don't care it's only been a few months. I want her. She's the one.* About two exits before the one leading to his parents' house, Grey made up his mind that he would have Carrie. She would be his wife no matter what the cost and he would not give up until she agreed. He took a deep breath and a temporary sense of peace settled over him. A small smile crept over his face.

He pulled into his parents large circular driveway and noticed his was the last car to arrive. *Good. Barbara is here. I can get some answers.* Checking his watch it was ten thirty and there were lights on only downstairs in the big Victorian house. Grey pulled out his key and opened the door.

As he stepped into the entryway, the buzz of voices stopped. He walked under the arch to the living room and his mother fairly jumped up from her chair, her face breaking into a huge smile.

"Grey! So happy to see you. Where is she? Still in the car, did she fall asleep?" His mother asked, her eyes darting around the entryway.

"She's not coming."

"What?" His mother said, sinking down into the sofa, her frown evaporating.

Grey looked directly at his sister, Barbara, and noticed she let out a big breath.

"Why? What happened? She's not sick is she?" Fran Andrews, Grey's mom, asked.

"No, she's not sick. Perhaps we'd better ask Barbara why Carrie's not here."

Jenna, John, his father and Fran all turned to look at Barbara. Even her husband, Earl, turned toward her. Barbara blushed.

"It's not my fault, Grey. Honestly." She sank down into a wing chair.

"She hasn't told me what happened. Would you?" Grey requested as he sat down in a wing chair across from her.

Barbara told her family the story about the conflict with her boss and the ad agency.

"And you were going to tell me about this, when?" Grey asked in angry tones, his face darkening.

"Honestly, Grey, I thought it didn't concern you. I mean the girl has to decide whether or not to keep her job or her boyfriend. Can you make that decision for her?"

Silence fell on the room.

"If I had known about it maybe I could..." he began.

"Maybe you could what?" Barbara said, rising from her chair.

"Discuss it with her?"

"If she wanted to discuss it with you, then why didn't she? This is all her choice, not mine." Barbara walked over to the fireplace, rested her hand on the mantle as she stared into the fire. "Do you think I want my little brother to lose the woman he loves?"

"Who said anything about love?"

"You invited her here, didn't you?"

"So?"

"So that says it all. Believe me, I didn't want to make that phone call. But I can't lose this job. Carrie is a very talented copywriter. I didn't want to lose her on our business either, but I had to call Goodhue." Barbara folded her arms across her chest and paced slowly in front of the fire.

"You wanted her to dump me so you could continue to have her on your account?" Grey questioned her, rising from his chair.

All eyes fell on Barbara.

"It wasn't a matter of what I wanted. It was her decision or Goodhue's. He could simply have fired her." She stopped moving and looked at each face staring at her.

"Or transferred her to another piece of business, maybe?"

"He said he didn't have anywhere else to put her."

"What about all that new business work she's doing?"

"There's no budget for salaries in new business. Since there's no income against that, they can't justify any salary expenses against it. Goodhue explained it all to me. Believe me, we discussed the options. I didn't want to put you in this position," Barbara said, putting her hand on his arm.

"You didn't put me anywhere, but you did jam up Carrie pretty badly."

"It's my boss. If I had my way..."

"I get it. I get it."

Grey strode out of the living room and back to his car. He opened the trunk and took out his bag. When he returned no one had moved from their spot and all were quiet.

"And Jenna gave her the thumbs up, too," sighed Colin, Grey's younger brother.

Colin got up and took empty coffee mugs into the kitchen. Jenna walked over to Grey and gave him a big hug. She whispered to him.

"You can't let her get away."

Grey looked at her.

"I want her in this family. I feel like she's my sister already."

"After one weekend?" He asked, raising an eyebrow.

"I like her. Besides, it wasn't an ordinary weekend," Jenna teased.

Grey put his hand up and stepped back.

"Okay, okay, I know... Please bring her back." Jenna placed her hand on his forearm.

Bill walked over to Jenna and took her hand, to lead her upstairs. Barbara walked by trying not to look at Grey on her way to the kitchen. John Andrews stopped and shook Grey's hand.

"Good to see you, son," he said before turning to go upstairs.

Fran hugged Grey.

"I know you're disappointed," Grey started.

"It's okay, dear. I'm fine. I want you to be happy. Resolve this in the best way for you."

His mother joined his father. Earl turned and waved a goodnight to Grey as he went to bed. Only Barbara was left in the kitchen.

Grey joined her, sitting down at the kitchen table.

"Coffee?" She asked, the pot poised over a clean mug.

He shook his head.

Barbara sat down across from him. "I'm sorry, Grey. If there was any other way..."

"It's not your fault, Barbara. You're right when you said Carrie should have discussed it with me. I don't know why she didn't."

"Good luck," she said, patting her brother on the arm.

"You coming to bed?" Earl asked, sticking his head in the kitchen.

Barbara got up and left with him.

Grey stood up and looked out the kitchen window over the sink. He watched the moon shine down on the bare branches of oak and maple trees covered with a light dusting of snow. In the moonbeams he could see snow falling. A white Thanksgiving, his favorite kind. He wouldn't be sharing it with Carrie. He missed her in this house. Everyone was going up to bed with someone and he wanted Carrie there, in his arms, in his bed. Disappointment welled up in his chest.

"This isn't over," he said aloud, to himself, before he went upstairs to bed.

# Chapter Fifteen

UNABLE TO SLEEP, CARRIE rose early on Thanksgiving Day. Even with friends bringing dishes, there was still a lot to do. She put up a big pot of coffee, made a list then sat down to her computer, she wanted to do a few edits and other tasks before beginning the job of preparing their meal.

An hour later Delia wandered down in her robe, yawning.

"I see you have things well in hand," she said, pouring herself a cup of coffee.

Next to a half-drunk mug of coffee was a chopping board and Carrie was busy making stuffing ingredients ready, chopping mushroom and celery.

"So much to do. Have to get organized."

"I'm so glad you can cook because, frankly, it's beyond me, Carrie. I never got the urge to learn. This will be our best Thanksgiving ever, now you're here."

Though it was only eight o'clock, the phone rang. Delia jumped.

"Who the hell can that be at this hour?"

She picked up the phone and cleared her throat. After greetings were exchanged, she took the phone into the living room and sat down on the sofa.

"Grey, how nice to hear from you," she purred.

Carrie's head shot up and she stared over the counter and pass through from the kitchen to the living room at Delia. Her aunt smiled back at her.

"She's here, but she's preparing our meal. I'm all thumbs in the kitchen. We're not having a big crowd. Just a few friends and my main squeeze, Tony. Oh, yes, and Tony's son, Mario. Mario's single, thirty and quite the Latin lover I hear."

Delia paused, listening.

"If she gets through soon, I'll have her call you. Have a wonderful holiday. Yes, you, too."

Delia hung up the phone.

"Why did you tell him about Mario?" Carrie asked, unable to keep the anger from her voice.

"The man should know who his competition is," Delia said, smiling.

GREY SLAMMED THE PHONE down, causing his father to turn around. John Andrews was minding a big pan of bacon on the stove while scrambling a dozen eggs. Other members of the Andrews family were getting dressed and dividing up chores.

John looked over at Grey with a quizzical expression.

"Nothing, Dad." Grey said in a clipped tone.

"Didn't sound like nothing to me."

"Delia's boyfriend has a thirty-year-old son...some Latin lover type. He's going to dinner there today."

"You can't be worried about Carrie and this guy, can you?"

Grey gave his father a stern look.

"She's that fickle, some guy she just meets sweeps her off her feet? Bosh!"

"That kind of thing happens all the time," Grey said, sinking down into a kitchen chair.

John turned off the heat under the bacon and turned to face his son.

"If that's what's worrying you, what are you doing here?"

Grey looked up at his dad.

"Son, is this your woman?" John turned his back to the stove and faced his son.

Grey nodded.

"Then go get her and stop bothering everyone. We have a Thanksgiving meal to make here. I have bacon to cook. Get outta here," he said, turning back to the stove not able to hide a smile from his son and put the heat back on the bacon.

Grey hung his head and smiled. He stood up, took his keys out of his pocket and moved toward the door, stopping at the stove.

"I think I need some air. Thanks, Dad," he said, clapping his father on the shoulder.

John simply smiled at his son and went back to tending his bacon.

The last thing Grey heard as he was closing the front door behind him was his father's voice calling out.

"Who's first for breakfast?"

CARRIE PICKED UP HER list with one hand and downed her second cup of coffee with the other. The turkey was in the oven. The table was set. The salad was tossed, waiting only for dressing to be added. Two pies were ready. Everything else was being brought by others.

Carrie opened her computer to go back to her edits while Delia took a shower. She sat at the dining room table and looked out the window. The wide stream out back had a thin layer of ice forming in spots. A light snow was falling and just enough was sticking to the branches of the evergreen trees to make them resemble the trees in a Currier & Ives Christmas card. The sight was beautiful, one she had enjoyed for many years when her family joined Delia and Jack at this cozy little house in the woods for a family Thanksgiving.

She wondered what Grey was doing, what his family was doing. She felt guilty about canceling at the last minute. What would they think of her rudeness? Surely Barbara would explain everything. Still, she had wanted to go, wanted to meet his family see their house that Grey raved about so often. They were probably all having fun, teasing each other, doing chores and playing games like every other big family on this holiday. Carrie felt a pang in her chest. *How wonderful to belong to a big family of loving people.* She sighed and stretched, unable to concentrate on her writing. *I'm taking today off.* She closed her computer and threw on fleece pants and a down jacket.

"I'm going for a walk, Delia," she shouted toward the bathroom.

Carrie picked up a handful of bird seed from the sack by the back door, went outside and, shut the door behind her.

Carrie wandered into the woods, looking for birds. Most had flown south but there were always a few sparrows and chickadees looking for food. She threw some bird seed on the ground and kept walking, her eyes searching for a large stump to sit down on. She found a trunk perpendicular to the ground where it had fallen after some storm or other and she sat down, watching for the birds to come eat.

A few did stop by and she pulled out her camera. She snapped a few good pictures of them picking up the seed. After about twenty minutes she started to get cold. Her fingertips and toes became uncomfortable as frostbite threatened. She started back to the house. When she looked up at the sky, she was surprised to see smoke coming from Delia's chimney.

*Who made a fire?* Maybe Delia had stopped being afraid of matches long enough to learn to lay a fire and light it but Carrie doubted it. Delia, such a talented woman in some areas, was never much of a homemaker. As she got closer to the house, Carrie noticed a car in Delia's driveway. Sure enough, it was a silver Jaguar XK.

She hurried into the house and stopped at the kitchen door to take her shoes off. She heard laughter coming from the living room and peeked out the pass-through to see Grey having coffee with Delia in the living room in front of a roaring fire most likely built by him. When Carrie entered the room, he stood up.

She looked at him wearing a tan vee-neck sweater over a white shirt, brown corduroy slacks and a big smile. Her heart did a flip. She couldn't believe how happy she was to see him.

"I've got some calls to make," Delia said and slipped quietly up the stairs to her room.

"Hi," Grey said, standing immobile in front of the sofa.

"Hi." Carrie returned, her feet riveted to the ground.

She wanted to run to him but didn't know how he felt.

"Did you talk to Barbara?" she asked.

He nodded.

"So you know everything," she said.

"Not everything. Don't know how you feel," he said, moving toward her slowly.

"Me?" She backed away a step.

"What are you going to do?" He continued to move toward her.

"I...I..."

"Maybe we should talk about it?"

"You drove all this way to talk?"

Grey crossed the room and was standing in front of her. She looked up into his eyes and couldn't speak. She couldn't believe how much she had missed him in since Monday when they were last together.

"I know this is a tough decision for you...and we haven't known each other for long. But I know how I feel about you, Carrie," Grey said.

"Do you?"

"We could move in together. I have plenty of room in my house. Space for you to write...you could have your own writing room."

"Move in together?" She wrapped her arms around her chest.

*Not what I wanted to hear.*

"I don't want to lose you."

He looked down at his hands, then his gaze went to the floor before it came up to rest on

her face.

"I've never made a commitment before. This isn't easy for me." His foot tapped on the floor.

"And I've been badly burned once, so commitment isn't easy for me either," she countered.

"What would it take for you to quit?" He reached out, his hand cupped her elbow.

"You make this sound like a business deal. Like I should name my price."

"I don't mean to. I...this is my first conversation...like this."

"Never wanted to before?" She stepped back away from him.

"Never wanted anyone the way I want you."

"You want me to quit?"

"I'd be lying if I said I didn't. Of course I want you to choose me. But because you want to. Because you love me the way I love you." A flush stole into his cheeks.

*There it is. The magic word. Love.*

As he moved closer, she grinned up at him. He placed his hands on her arms and lowered his head until his lips were only a breath away from hers.

"I do love you, Grey. More than I thought."

"I love you so much, Carrie. These past two days without you, I've been...nuts...miserable. I adore you. I need you with me. Marry me."

He retrieved a small box from his pants pocket and flicked it open with his thumb to reveal a stunning marquis shaped diamond solitaire about three carats.

Carrie's jaw fell open as she stared at the ring, then at him, then at the ring again.

"Well?" he asked, beads of sweat breaking out on his forehead.

"Yes...yes! I will," she choked out, emotion closing her throat.

Grey's face lit up with a huge grin. He took the ring out of the box and slipped it on her finger.

"It's beautiful," she said, spreading the fingers of her left hand, watching the ring sparkle in the glow from the fire.

"And so are you," he said, his mouth descending on hers for a passionate kiss.

Carrie wound her arms around his neck and pulled herself closer to him. His hands traveled down her back to squeeze her behind. When they broke, she stepped back, her finger touched her lower lip.

"I love you so much...I've missed you, too."

"Why didn't you call?"

"I needed to think this through before I made a decision. I didn't know what would happen between us. If I quit my job and you disappeared then I would be...devastated."

"Now you can quit and not worry. I'm not going anywhere. Go ahead. Call Goodhue. Drop the bomb on him today," Grey urged.

"I don't have to."

He shot her a questioning look.

"I already did. I faxed him my resignation this morning."

"You did? Before you knew for certain about me? Oh, Carrie...you do love me, don't you?" He pulled her into his arms again.

She closed her eyes and sank into his warmth. "I couldn't leave you. I figured if you left me, I'd deal, somehow."

"I'll never leave you."

"I know, I'm on 'The Marriage List', right?"

"What list?"

They laughed and hugged again. Delia appeared on the stairs. "So, you two reconciled, eh?"

"We're engaged." Grey beamed at her.

"It's about time!" Delia said, pretending to wipe her brow.

"Now you can tell Mario, 'tough luck.'"

"Mario? Mario's gay," Delia chuckled.

The surprised look on Grey's face made both women laugh.

"Delia, you lied to me!"

"Not exactly, Grey. He is a Latin lover, but with men, not women. I decided to leave that part out."

"The turkey's in the oven and everything else is done here, right? If you want to leave, tell me what to do with the blasted bird and go ahead."

"Sure?"

"Of course, Cookie. I'd never stand in the way of true love."

Carrie wrote down instructions, threw her clothes in her bag and ran out to the car. It was already twelve o'clock and they had another two hours or more on the road. Carrie slid into the seat next to him, fastened her seatbelt and sank back. She couldn't stop smiling. She turned to look at Grey's profile. He glanced at her, flashing a beaming smile and she giggled.

Happiness washed over her as the XK flew down the highway. It seemed like most people had reached their destinations for the day because the roads were empty.

"Will your parents be mad?"

"My mother has been waiting for you since I was twenty-five, honey."

"I can't wait to meet your family and see that fabulous house."

"It pales compared to you." He glanced at her for a moment.

"Spoken like a man in love."

She glanced out the window, feeling the rapid beat of her heart.

"Now I can spend my time writing fiction."

"I have the perfect room for you. It's on the second floor faces south, gets the morning sun. You can sit in there and write all day long. No more new business pitches, late nights…except with me, of course,"

"I'm moving into your townhouse?"

"Of course, you're going to be my wife. I love your apartment, but it's too small for the two of us…and eventually the three or more of us."

"Children?"

"How many?"

"Two?" She held up two fingers and shot him a questioning glance.

"Sounds good to me," He chuckled.

Carrie couldn't get over how high she felt…floating on air.

THE XK PULLED UP IN front of the imposing three story Victorian house at about two thirty in the afternoon. Grey chuckled to himself assuming all the chores had been done and he managed to skip out on all of them.

When they got out of the car, he glanced at the house and saw the entire family crowded around the two giant living room windows peeking through the drapes. He smiled at their eagerness. Grey went to the truck and picked up Carrie's suitcase. When he turned around, she was there, slipping her hand in his. He laced his fingers with hers. She wore a frown.

"Nervous?"

"A little."

"Don't be. You can't possibly be as nervous as they are," he said, indicating the house with a nod of his head.

As they approached the house, Grey saw his mother disappear from the window first, then each family member peeled away from the glass and filed into the large entry way to descend on Carrie when they walked in.

The door opened before they even reached the front steps and his mother stood, her arms folded across her chest as it was cold out with a big smile lighting up her face. Grey's eyes locked with hers and the smile on his face grew to match hers.

"This must be Carrie," Fran Andrews said, opening her arms.

She drew Carrie in right away, engulfing her in a warm hug. Carrie smiled and closed her eyes.

"Good guess, Mom," Grey teased.

"Come inside, come inside, it's cold out there," Grey's father insisted, pulling on his son's arm, reaching for Carrie's bag

"I've got it, Dad." Grey held onto the bag as his father backed into the house.

The rest of the family was huddled by the front door. Jenna pushed through the crowd to be the next to hug Carrie. She pushed back from her and grabbed Carrie's hand. Jenna's gaze took in the large diamond ring. She shrieked.

"You're engaged?" Jenna jumped up in the air.

Carrie moved to Grey's side, slipping her arm around his waist and smiled.

"Had to propose or lose this one. Now she's mine." He smiled down at her, placing his arm around Carrie's shoulders.

Fran Andrews wiped a tear from her eye. "Come in, Carrie. Grey, take her bag up to your room. Dinner won't be until five o'clock. But we have some nibbles in here." Fran took Carrie by the hand and guided her into the living room.

"Don't think we didn't save some chores for you, Grey," Colin shouted.

"Thanks, Colin!" Grey hollered back from the hall.

When he came down the stairs and turned into the living room, he stopped at the archway. His heart leaped at the scene before his eyes. Carrie was on the sofa and the rest of the family was huddled around. Jenna had claimed the seat next to Carrie. Fran was on the other side. His father sat next to Barbara on a loveseat. The in-laws took club chairs and Colin sat on the ottoman near the sofa. Everyone was talking, shooting questions at Carrie too fast for her to answer. She was laughing.

When he came into the room, they quieted down for a moment and looked at him. *I have a lot to be thankful for this year.*

"One at a time, one at a time. Give her a chance to breathe," he said, sinking down next to her in the space made by Jenna who straddled the arm of the sofa right behind Grey.

Carrie looked up at him and he brought his mouth down for a quick kiss.

"Hey, wait for mistletoe, horny guy," Colin piped up.

# Chapter Sixteen

NOVEMBER TWENTY-THIRD, the day before their fourth Thanksgiving together, was cold and rainy. Remembering back to their first Thanksgiving together, Carrie gazed at her engagement ring, now nestled comfortably against a matching wedding band for the past three years. She sat by the full length window facing the charming backyard of their townhouse on Manhattan Avenue_. Cold rain drizzled down the windows making the view fuzzy. Carrie sat warm and cozy in fleece pants and shirt sipping a cup of hot tea, watching the occasional bird stop at their feeder.

Tonight she and Grey were going to cook together for tomorrow's feast. They were scheduled to leave at seven o'clock in the morning to arrive in time for the Andrews' family Thanksgiving breakfast. It would have to be an early night for them.

Grey was at a business meeting, an unexpected one that arose from a new business opportunity too good to pass up. She stretched out and put the cup down, picking up her red pen. She was editing her third mystery novel but felt restless. Where was Grey? She missed him. He had been so preoccupied with this new deal they had not spent much time together in the past week. Carrie felt sexy, desire tingling inside her. She needed Grey. They hadn't made love in over a week, the longest they had gone in their three married years, and she felt itchy.

She got an idea how to bring him home. She looked at her watch, jumped up from her chair, grabbed her cell phone and headed to their bedroom where she stripped off her shirt and bra. Facing the large dresser mirror, she stuck several coy poses. Aiming the phone camera, she took a picture of her naked breasts, as close up as she could get. She checked her watch. *Right now, in the middle of his meeting.* She smiled as she sent the photo to his phone with the words, "missing you, hurry home for a good time." Then she lay down on the bed and giggled.

GREY LOOKED AT HIS watch as his partner broached another question to the president of the company they were considering investing in. It was four o'clock and he needed to get home. He missed Carrie. He was horny, restless and wanted to leave but the president droned on. In his pocket, his cell phone vibrated.

He excused himself and went into the hall to retrieve the message. It was from Carrie. As soon as he saw the picture and read the note, he burst out laughing. He looked at it several times feeling desire course through his veins before clicking his phone shut. His luscious wife was waiting for him. Time to leave the meeting and return home.

He sent a text back to her, "On my way, don't start without me."

Taking a minute to compose himself and wipe the lustful grin off his face before returning to the conference room, Grey stopped at the water fountain and took a deep breath.

"Gentleman, I have an urgent call from home, so I must leave you," Grey said.

"Carrie? Is everything all right?"

"Nothing serious, John, but something that needs my immediate attention."

Grey worked hard to keep the smile off his lips and succeeded until he reached the parking lot where he broke into a huge grin. The XK couldn't jump over the cars, so the slow trip home from downtown Manhattan took forty-five minutes instead of the usual twenty. He texted Carrie back every fifteen minutes but the frustration of the stop-and-go day-before-Thanksgiving traffic, put him on edge.

When he finally arrived home, Carrie was on the phone with Delia. He caught the tail end of her conversation.

"I have the last item on my list, Delia...Oops, Grey's home, gotta go."

She hung up the phone and turned to him with a guilty look.

"Did I hear the word 'list'? You have a list?" he asked, raising his eyebrows while he took the glass of cabernet sauvignon she handed him.

Carrie wore a cream-colored, short negligee with a matching silk robe over it. She blushed a becoming shade of pink.

"A marriage list?"

"After you came up with your list, I thought it was a good idea. So I started one, too." Carrie tucked one leg under her and sank down on the sofa.

"And all this time you didn't tell me because...?"

"You never asked."

"But once you knew..."

"I suppose I should have."

"A marriage list?"

"It started out that way. After we got engaged, there was only one thing left on the list. And today, my final wish came true."

"One wish? And what might that be?" Grey knelt down on the sofa, looming over her, desire in his eyes.

She looked up at him, opening her robe. His hands slid the sleeves down over her arms and off. He leaned over and nibbled on her neck. She closed her eyes, feeling the heat from his lips travel to her core.

"I'm waiting," he whispered in her ear as he proceeded to yank his tie loose and unbutton his shirt.

Carrie helped him by unzipping his pants.

"You are going to tell me aren't you?"

"Thinking about it." A devilish smile played at her lips.

"Soon, please, before we get preoccupied."

He moved back and stood up to slide his pants and boxers to the floor then returned to the sofa. Kneeling over her, he untied the bow holding the negligee together so his hands could massage her breasts.

"There's something different about you but first, give. What's the last thing."

He buried his face in her neck, awaiting her response.

"The last thing on my list was to get pregnant," she whispered in his ear.

Grey froze in position, then picked his head up as his eyes searched hers.

"You're pregnant?" His eyes wide, his lips breaking into a grin.

She smiled and nodded "I found out today."

"Another dream come true," he said as she pulled him down on top of her.

# **THE END**

# About the Author

JEAN JOACHIM IS A BEST-selling romance fiction author, with books hitting the Top 100 list since 2012. She writes contemporary romance, which includes sports romance and romantic suspense.

*Dangerous Love Lost & Found,* First Place winner in the 2015 Oklahoma Romance Writers of America, International Digital Award contest. *The Renovated Heart* won Best Novel of the Year from Love Romances Café. *Lovers & Liars* was a RomCon finalist in 2013. And *The Marriage List* tied for third place as Best Contemporary Romance from the Gulf Coast RWA.

To Love or Not to Love tied for second place in the 2014 New England Chapter of Romance Writers of America Reader's Choice contest.

She was chosen Author of the Year in 2012 by the New York City chapter of RWA.

Married and the mother of two sons, Jean lives in New York City. Early in the morning, you'll find her at her computer, writing, with a cup of tea, and a secret stash of black licorice.

Jean has 30+ books, novellas and short stories published.

Sign up for her newsletter, on her website, and be eligible for her private paperback sales.

# Books by Jean C. Joachim

**<u>BOTTOM OF THE NINTH</u>**
DAN ALEXANDER, PITCHER
MATT JACKSON, CATCHER
JAKE LAWRENCE, THIRD BASEMAN
NAT OWEN, FIRST BASE (Coming)
BOBBY HERNANDEZ, SECOND BASE (Coming)
SKIP QUINCY, SHORTSTOP (Coming)
EXTRA INNINGS (Coming)

**<u>FIRST & TEN SERIES</u>**
GRIFF MONTGOMERY, QUARTERBACK
GRIFF MONTGOMERY, QUARTERBACK (EDIZIONE ITAL-
IANA)
BUDDY CARRUTHERS, WIDE RECEIVER
PETE SEBASTIAN, COACH
DEVON DRAKE, CORNERBACK
SLY "BULLHORN" BRODSKY, OFFENSIVE LINE
AL "TRUNK" MAHONEY, DEFENSIVE LINE
HARLEY BRENNAN, RUNNING BACK
OVERTIME, THE FINAL TOUCHDOWN
A KING'S CHRISTMAS
TUFFER'S CHRISTMAS WISH (Short Story)
**<u>THE MANHATTAN DINNER CLUB</u>**
RESCUE MY HEART

SEDUCING HIS HEART
SHINE YOUR LOVE ON ME
TO LOVE OR NOT TO LOVE

**<u>HOLLYWOOD HEARTS SERIES</u>**

IF I LOVED YOU
RED CARPET ROMANCE
MEMORIES OF LOVE
MOVIE LOVERS
LOVE'S LAST CHANCE
LOVERS & LIARS
HIS LEADING LADY (Series Starter)

**<u>NOW AND FOREVER SERIES</u>**

NOW AND FOREVER 1, A LOVE STORY
NOW AND FOREVER 2, THE BOOK OF DANNY
NOW AND FOREVER 3, BLIND LOVE
NOW AND FOREVER 4, THE RENOVATED HEART
NOW AND FOREVER 5, LOVE'S JOURNEY
NOW AND FOREVER, CALLIE'S STORY (prequel)

**<u>MOONLIGHT SERIES</u>**

SUNNY DAYS, MOONLIT NIGHTS
APRIL'S KISS IN THE MOONLIGHT
UNDER THE MIDNIGHT MOON
MOONLIGHT & ROSES (prequel)

**<u>LOST & FOUND SERIES</u>**

LOVE, LOST AND FOUND
DANGEROUS LOVE, LOST AND FOUND

**<u>NEW YORK NIGHTS NOVELS</u>**

THE MARRIAGE LIST
THE LOVE LIST
THE DATING LIST

**<u>SHORT STORIES</u>**

SWEET LOVE REMEMBERED

THE SECOND-PLACE HEART (Coming)
THE HOUSE-SITTER'S CHRISTMAS

# Don't miss out!

Click the button below and you can sign up to receive emails whenever Jean Joachim publishes a new book. There's no charge and no obligation.

https://books2read.com/r/B-A-LBKB-AHSE

Connecting independent readers to independent writers.

www.ingramcontent.com/pod-product-compliance
Lightning Source LLC
Chambersburg PA
CBHW050542190726
48284CB00003B/1175